FOUR CORNERS, VOLUME 1

Theodore Roscoe

FOUR CORNERS

VOLUME 1

THEODORE ROSCOE

ALTUS PRESS
2015

EDITED AND DESIGNED BY
Matthew Moring

PUBLISHING HISTORY

"He Took Richmond" originally appeared in the June 5, 1937 issue of *Argosy* magazine (Vol. 273, No. 4). Copyright © 1937 by The Frank A. Munsey Company. Copyright renewed © 1964 and assigned to Steeger Properties, LLC. All rights reserved.

"Frivolous Sal" originally appeared in the July 17, 1937 issue of *Argosy* magazine (Vol. 274, No. 4). Copyright © 1937 by The Frank A. Munsey Company. Copyright renewed © 1964 and assigned to Steeger Properties, LLC. All rights reserved.

"Barber, Barber, Shave a Pig" originally appeared in the August 7, 1937 issue of *Argosy* magazine (Vol. 275, No. 1). Copyright © 1937 by The Frank A. Munsey Company. Copyright renewed © 1964 and assigned to Steeger Properties, LLC. All rights reserved.

"I Was the Kid with the Drum" originally appeared in the October 30, 1937 issue of *Argosy* magazine (Vol. 277, No. 1). Copyright © 1937 by The Frank A. Munsey Company. Copyright renewed © 1964 and assigned to Steeger Properties, LLC. All rights reserved.

"Daisies Won't Tell" originally appeared in the January 8, 1938 issue of *Argosy* magazine (Vol. 278, No. 5). Copyright © 1938 by The Frank A. Munsey Company. Copyright renewed © 1965 and assigned to Steeger Properties, LLC. All rights reserved.

THANKS TO
Joel Frieman, Chris Kalb, and Gerd Pircher

ISBN
978-1-61827-186-0

Visit *altuspress.com* for more books like this.
Printed in the United States of America.

TABLE OF CONTENTS

I

HE TOOK RICHMOND

A Novelette for Decoration Day.

CHAPTER I

FOUR CORNERS MAY not be as big as New York, but it has as much civic pride. The sign beyond the bridge says *Watch Us Grow* and the trout fishing down by Peterson's Mill is the sort that lures even the tall hats from Broadway. Come off-season it's pretty quiet, but we have our doings—barn dances over at the Grange, husking bees, meetings at Legion Hall over Clapp's Feed Store to see about someday erecting a monument to the boys who went Over There. There's the Armistice Day celebration at Brockton, and ten of our boys parade, and the whole town goes over with them to see them do it—I mean, the *whole* town. You can understand, then, how a place as public spirited as Four Corners would feel about an embarrassment like Anecdote Jones.

"Disgrace, that's what he is."

"Public nuisance. Oughta someone take him in hand."

"Sits there right where all the toorists goin' by can't help but see him. T'bacca juice a-runnin', on th' bench there whittlin' an' tellin' that loony yarn of his'n—"

"Dunno why Lem ever took him on at th' garage. Reckon he just walked in on Lem one day, an' Lem hadn't got the courage to turn th' poor old critter out."

"They do say he's kinda *a*-gile with a repair kit, 'f he'd ever stop whittlin' an' keep his mind on what he's doin'. Lem don't pay him nothin'. Look, he's over there now—"

The old man paused to drive a squirt of brown juice ten feet to mid-road where it bounced on the dusty concrete. His eyes—cups of blue evening mist in a face as stained and weathered as aged vellum—did not see the highroad or the red front of Clapp's Feed Store across the way or the far frost-tinted hills of Vermont that kept Canada out of the valley. Neither were they aware of this garage-front setting—*Let Lem Fix It*—the Mocony gasoline pump, the oil-splotched driveway under the spreading chestnut tree, or the group standing close around.

"I c'n see him now, just like it was yest'd'y. Standin' right in front of me, no farther'n *that*. Yes, sir, with his beard an' his old slouch hat an' his cigar puffin' away like a trench mortar in the wilderness, 'Jonesey,' he says to me—he allus called me Jonesey, just like him an' me was equals—'Jonesey,' he says, 'I want you should take some boys up to that'ere pine knoll, an' hang onter it,' he says. 'Hang onter it like a bulldog to a rott,' he says chewin' th' cigar 'tween his teeth, ashes goin' all down his coat, 'because if th' Johnny Rebs drive you off'n that knoll they may get a rider through to Johnston's Army in North Caroliny, an' Johnston'll come a-runnin' to join Lee an' we'll never take Richmond,' he says. 'It's just like one link in a big chain, Jonesey,' he says, 'but it's a mighty im-*portant* link. You hold that pine knoll tonight, an' it means we're in Richmond tomorrow,' he says. 'You do that, Jonesey, an' it'll be just like you took Richmond yourself,' he says."

The old man nodded to himself in memory; eased his position on the bench, and shaved a delicate curl from the latest one of the endless series of big forked sticks he's always whittling as he talks.

"That piney hilltop," his voice quavered on, "that knoll up there was just about like an island settin' up above a hull sea of Rebs. Be a big fight to hold it, I c'd see that. 'But I'll try,' I says. 'You want it held, Gen'ral; I'll sure make a try.' And do you know what Grant done then? Put his hand on my shoulder, he did. Right on my shoulder! Gen'ral *Grant!* 'Jonesey,' he says, 'try *hell!* You *gotta* hold that knoll till morning,' he says. 'Don't you

wanta some day be able to say that you was the man who took Richmond—'"

THE OLD MAN jammed the forked stick he'd been whittling into a lumpy hip pocket, and gently placed his hand on his left shoulder while his eyes bleared and dreamed. High in the afternoon sky some geese were honking.

Jim Hardy snickered and nudged Mule Lickett. Charlie Rambow chuckled. But Andrew Dobbs grunted impatiently and looked in embarrassment at the city man standing near the gas pump. This city feller would think Four Corners was a hick town, the sort of place where they were still talking about the Civil War. It was especially annoying when all the boys were in their new Legion uniforms—Bowd Post—for the parade and field day over at Brockton. Jim and Mule and Andrew had even been in the A.E.F. They looked pretty nifty in their new outfits—chromium trench helmets, orange tunics, horizon blue britches with scarlet braid. Andrew tried to think of something to say to the city man. Only Johnny Lane, the kid in brown overalls, tinkering at the engine of the city man's big olive sedan, straightened up and turned to listen.

"It was 1865," the old man was going on, "an' I'll never fergit it, Grant puttin' his hand on my shoulder, sayin', 'Jonesey, you gotta hold that knoll—'"

"And did you hold it?" the city man said with a yawn.

"We ain't got to that yet," the old man said, and there was a trace of querulous asperity in his creaking voice. He was worrying a slab of cut plug, and a little trickle of tobacco juice was leaking down through the white quills on his trembling chin. "But I and the boys"—transferring the stain from chin to wrist—"I and the boys got up there on th' knoll, an' you could plumb see th' rooftops o' Richmond from there, too. Well, it's quiet as you please for a spell, an' just about sundown I'm thinkin' maybe them Rebs ain't gonna make a try to break through. Then next thing you know there's a bay'net charge. Charge? Twenty of us boys up there, at th' start of that first attack. Ten of us when it's over. Them Rebels got close enough, b'gee, to put a bay'net clean through my hat. I got th' hat"—the old man eyed his audience hopefully—"to prove it."

No one asked him to prove it. Andrew Dobbs snapped at him, "Listen, Anecdote! Go tell Lem we're waitin' for him out here, an' to jump into it or we'll be late for th' parade!"

The old man didn't hear. He went on dreamily, "That wasn't th' only attack. Them Rebs kept a-comin' an' a-comin'. Finally there's only five of us boys left. Then three. Then just me an' a youngster no more'n a kid. But we'd give them Johnny Rebs somethin' to chaw on, too. Moon come up, an' we held 'em off. Snipin'. Shot plenty them gray Secessionists. Reckon' they figger we got an army up there, so they give us everything they got. All th' sudden—*bang!* Like that! Grape. Cannister. Lead. Minnie ball. Bullets an' round-shot flyin' like a blizzard, till th' thunder like to split your skull!"

Charlie Rambow rolled a little flimflam on the snare drum attached to his belt. Charlie's the Bowd Post drummer, and he's a wit, too. *Rat-ta-tat-tat.* Softly. He grinned, "Was it loud as that, Anecdote?"

"Louder," the old man snapped. "Like to make your nose bleed from th' roar."

"And did you take Richmond?" the city man asked, idly.

"I run outa bullets," the old man husked. "Boy with me was killed, an' I run clean outa bullets."

"But you held the piney knoll?" the city man smiled, amused. He was a smooth-looking man in a belted camel's hair topcoat, derby hat, butter-colored pigskin gloves. Suggestive of fast cars and horses. Enviously, Andrew Dobbs would have liked to talk with him.

"Honest, mister," he interrupted with an irritated gesture. "Don't let old Anecdote bother you. He'd gab here for th' next six hours." Andrew tapped his forehead and winked suggestively. The city man grinned.

"Go ahead, Pop," the city man reminded. "You're out of bullets, surrounded, alone on the knoll. How'd you make out?"

"I held 'em off," the old man panted. "The Rebs kept comin', but I held 'em off. All alone in them pine on the hill. Last man left. Every one o' my comrades was killed."

"Tenting tonight on the old camp ground," Jim Hardy snickered.

"He was outa bullets, but he held 'em off," Mule nodded.

"And he didn't get no reinforcements from Grant, neither," Andrew Dobbs put in with mock gravity, seeing that the city man was entertained.

"Yes, sir, that's how it was!" Old Anecdote's hands were trembling excitedly on his thin knees. "No reinforcements, 'cause th' Rebs were attackin' down th' rest of th' battle field. An' there I was isolated, marooned-like. Me agin' all them gray devils. Moon was up, an' I see 'em comin' uphill through th' bushes, scattered out, jumpin' from bush to bush. One after another they're comin'. But I think of what Gen'ral Grant says to me, I think of how he put his hand right on my shoulder, I—well, I just *had* t'hold that knoll."

"But how did you hold it?" the city man wanted to know.

"Eh?"

"You were out of bullets. Surrounded. How did you hold the hill?"

A puzzled wrinkle creased the old vellum forehead. The watery eyes, coming back into focus with the present, surveyed the audience in dismay. The old man fumbled at his chin, looking about helplessly.

"How did I—How did I *hold* the hill—?"

A ROAR of laughter convulsed Jim Hardy and Mule Lickett. Charlie Rambow whistled *Tramp, Tramp, Tramp, The Boys Are Marching.* Only Johnny Lane, looking up from the unhooded engine, called, "Aw, why don'tya leave him alone?" and then the doors slammed wide open in the garage front, and Lem came out in his captain's uniform, dusting his sleeves. Businesslike and in a hurry, Lem was.

"Sorry," he told the city man. "I can't find the part to fit your carburetor on that make of car. Garage at Brockton hasn't got one either. Afraid you'll just have to wait till Johnny can make you a piece. Hustle it up for th' gentleman, Johnny. All right, boys"—pointing to the flivver parked at road's edge—"rest of th' town will have got there ahead of us. Let's go."

Uniforms jingling, they piled into the Model T.

"G'bye, Anecdote!" Charlie Rambow played a roll on the snare drum. "Sounded just like you was in a real war, eh, Anecdote?"

"Real war?" the old man creaked to his feet; shook an impotent fist at the grinning faces. "Listen, you dang whippersnappers in yer dang soldier suits. Think y're all a'mighty smart, don't you! Lemme tell you, soldiers back in *my* day didn't have no time fer wearin' fancy clothes. Hand to hand, we had to fight in *my* day. You fellers just sat around all dressed up in yer trenches, hidin' behind a lotta bob wire—"

"Ever hear of gas, an' airyplanes, an' machine-guns, Anecdote?"

"We fought with our hands," the old man shrilled windily.

"We didn't hunker down behind a lotta gol dang machinery, waitin' scairt green fer some gun fifty miles away to blow us to pieces. We *seen* the men we was fightin'! Hand to hand, my day. Use yer head, too. In-*dividuals,* not a gol-dern *mass!* Tell a man to hold a hill, he held it—!"

"Tell us sometime how you took Richmond, Anecdote!"

The flivver, having caught St. Vitus, was starting off. Old Anecdote waved outraged fists at the taunting occupants. "G'wan," he shrilled. "G'wan to yer pee-rade! Think y're such dang good fightin' men these days—whyn't you rid th' country of these hoodlums like that Joe Gravatti kidnaper runnin' loose everywhere with his gang?" Doddering to the road edge, he screeched after the departing car, "Yaah—you spent more time with yer wonderful shootin' irons, an' less time paradin' over to Brockton in yer bright pants, our country'd be a sight better off!"

Airyplanes! Gas! Machine-guns! Eyes glazed with indignation, Old Anecdote trudged shakily, mutteringly, into the dim seclusion of the garage; blundered up the steep flight of steps to the loft above, where charity had awarded his years with an iron cot, a spittoon, a nail to hang his belongings on, and a job that consisted of gluing patches on worn-out inner tubes.

He slammed the trap door as angrily as he could; teetered through a rubbish of old tires, tubes, nuts, bolts, dead storage batteries and other bits of junk discarded by an extravagant motor industry; and opened the tight little window, hardly wide enough for a pigeon to get through, that overlooked driveway and gas pump below.

Late sunlight sifted into the darkness around him; he pulled up a cracker box, picked up an inner tube to start a patch. But he sat with the tube forgotten in wrinkled hands, his eyes fixed wistfully on an old slouch hat, a cobwebby ghost of a hat on the wall above him.

"Soldiers!" he snapped *"Them!"*

CHAPTER II

AFTER A WHILE his embittered glance shifted to the window, looked down on the driveway below, the big sedan down there, the gas pump. Johnny Lane was having a hard time repairing the big sedan's engine. Johnny Lane, the old man reflected, was all right. Respectful to an old man.

Johnny Lane's voice drifted up in the cooling dusk.

"That's Anecdote Jones, yes, sir. Oh, yes, sir, harmless—must be ninety years old, pretty near. Ain't no one in the village can remember when he came here—they like to kid him, y'see, but I kinda feel sorry for an old man; his mind goes like that. Allus thinkin' he took Richmond like he says, an' then when you ask him *how*, he can't never quite remember. All the time I've known him, I've never yet heard th' end of that yarn—allus gets that far, an' stops. Sort of—"The voice broke off. "Say, lookit that car comin' up th' road!"

The thin, fine roar of a high-powered motor drilled through the valley stillness. *Zzzzmmmmmmm!* Coming from the east and coming fast. Old Anecdote craned from the window and saw the car flash across the bridge. Durn fool, drivin' into a village like that! Lucky everybody'd gone t' Brockton, they might git run down—'cept th' constable oughta be here to arrest such joy riders. Old Anecdote jerked back his head. "Criminy!"

The car had come roaring like a cannon ball, slewed danger-ously into the driveway, brake-shrieked to a halt beside the Mocony gas pump. A sleek black touring sedan with New York plates. Men were piling from the car, a great fat man, two thin men, a short dark man, and a woman in a purple sweater with a floppy hat pulled way over one eye. Golly, the woman was smoking a cigar! There was somebody sick, too—a young girl about twelve with infantile, it looked— No, they had to lift her out of the car because her feet and hands—Anecdote stared in astonishment—were tied! And the fat man was holding a queer sort of gun that looked like a cross between a rifle and a big pistol. The short man was holding a shotgun. The woman had a revolver. The two thin men were half carrying the young girl, who seemed to have fainted. They all ran around the gas pump toward the city man who was standing there.

The fat man barked at the city man, "All set, Julius?"

The city man said, "All set."

Johnny Lane ran around from the front of the city man's car. He stopped in surprise at sight of the guns. "Say, what is this?"

"This is what," said the city man. Something metallic glinted in his grip; he struck out hard and hit Johnny Lane between the eyes. Johnny Lane dropped and writhed on the gravel, then drew up one knee and turned over on his side with his arms over his eyes.

"There ain't a man left in the village," the city man was saying. "They all went to that hick affair over at Brockton. I snipped the phone service. You put up those *Road Closed* signs at the fork?" He pointed a thumb at the highway.

"Yeah, and there ain't a bull on our trail," the fat man yelled. "Let's go! Into the garage!" Boots pounded in the dusk. They were carrying the girl in. Old Anecdote swung from the window and ran on funny legs to the stairway going down from the loft. A thin man poked a head through the trap opening, and pointed a short-barreled rifle.

"Stick 'em up, Methusalem! I got you covered!"

OLD ANECDOTE didn't know when he'd been so insulted. He couldn't understand why the young girl was tied up like that, or why the city man had hit Johnny Lane like that or why they'd tied Johnny up and propped him in a corner of the repair room with the girl. When he started to ask a question, the thin man who'd made him come down from the loft, poked him in the ribs with the gun and told him to shut-up-Methusalem.

Everything was queer. All these people seemed angry and hurried; everybody was excited, making quick jerky movements. The fat man was trotting all around the garage, poking his odd gun into doorways and peering into corners. The woman, all the while smoking that cigar, shamelessly peeled off her sweater and climbed into a black dress. Outside, the short dark man was bringing an armload of suitcases from the New York sedan. Everybody was swearing and hustling.

Old Anecdote was frightened and confused. He'd thought at first these people must be hunters—certain times of year there were lots of city folks turned up with rifles and shot-guns—but he could recall no hunting party like this one. What dang queer names, for example. The fat man they called Chief or Boss. Julius was all right for the city sharper, but the thin man who'd bullied him down the steps was named Gum-boils, and the second thin man was Skull. The swarthy short man's name was Dynamite, and the woman with the cigar was Toots. Old Anecdote couldn't understand their language, either.

When old Anecdote reached the ground floor, the skinny man behind him yelled, "Look what I found in the attic!"

Jumping around, gun aimed, the fat man snarled, "What t'hell!"

"Don't worry about him, Boss," the city man said. "He ain't there. He's lost some of his buttons."

Not there? Lost some of his buttons? The old man's eyes wandered in bewilderment. "Wha—what're you doin' here in Lem's ga-rage? Lem won't like it if—"

"Frisk him!" the fat man barked.

Old Anecdote received another poke. Too outraged for speech, he stood trembling in anger while Gum-boils slapped at his pockets and rummaged in his threadbare coat. "Nuts," the thin man grinned, bringing a handful of rusty nuts, washers and bolts out of one ragtag pocket. "Yeah, an' screwy, too. This mummy ain't packin' no rod."

"What's that on his hip?"

It was only one of the forked sticks he'd been whittling. The thin man returned it contemptuously, as an adult might give back to a child his toy, but found and took away the jackknife. "That's mine." The old man grabbed.

"You might cut yourself." Gum-boils pushed him off. "Okay, Chief, he's laundered. What you want done with him?"

"I know what I'd do with him," the woman with the cigar growled. Her lips pursed and went, "Pop!" ejecting a little burst of smoke.

The fat man's eyeballs, gooseberries set in cups of sour milk, surveyed old Anecdote suspiciously. "You!" he jabbed out. "Whatcha doin' here? Whatsa you' name?"

Old Anecdote squared his shoulders stiffly. "So ye don't know about it, eh? I guess maybe y'ain't never read about it, then. I'll tell you who I am, mister. I'm th' man who took Richmond!"

"Took who?" The fat eyelids squinted.

"He hasn't any roof," the city man advised the fat man. "He's a dim bulb, Chief. He ain't got any memory. Th' grease monkey was tellin' me. He can't remember nothing past the Civil War."

"Grant"—Old Anecdote nodded brightly—"Grant put his hand right on my shoulder, Yes, sir! *Gen'ral* Grant!"

"General Grant, phooey!" The fat man put his own hand on old Anecdote's shoulder; shoved him rudely against the wall.

Old Anecdote protested, "Here, that's no way to talk about—"

"You," the gooseberry eyes glared, "can the chatter!"

"Think I'm afraid of ye?" the old man shrilled, aware now of open hostility. "Think a man who stood off a hull batch o' Johnny Rebs an' held onter a pine knoll all night, same's if I took Richmond all by myself—think I'm afraid o' one of ye?"

"Shut up!" The meat reddened dangerously on the beefy forehead. "Shut up, you, or I'll blow you away!"

"I ain't afraid of yer goldang modern guns an' war gadgets, mister. I know ye," the old man squealed. "Y're one o' this here smart young gen'ration think y're a heap better'n they was in my day. Just 'cause y're totin' that new-fangled shootin' iron o' yourn. Lemme tell you, mister—"

"*Madonna!* I am to be told something by this clinking sack of bones!"

The woman with the cigar in her teeth was sliding shut the sheet-iron doors at the garage entry. She snarled over her shoulder, "Aw, give him a dose of tin, Chief." With the doors closed it was almost dark in the garage.

"I ain't afraid!" Old Anecdote's teeth were chattering on all six. "I wasn't afraid that night front o' Richmond, neither. Grant says, 'Jonesey, you gotta hold that there hill; don't let nobody break through.' I held 'er, too. Surrounded. My comrades lyin' shot dead. All by myself, I was, an' I I c'd see them gray Rebs a-comin' up—me up there outa bullets—"

"Only the pity of heaven," the fat man said, "keeps me right now from seeing that you are not out of bullets!"

"I ain't scairt a mite," old Anecdote panted. "Not of your kind, I ain't. Just gimme a comp'ny of Federals, that's all—gimme *one* Federal—he'd knock th' tarnation daylights outa such as you—"

"*Federals!*" the word and the fat man's breath hit old Anecdote's face like a gust from a gas main. "Federals, is it?" Eyes glittering, he jabbed the snub-nosed gun into the old man's wishbone, fastening him against the brick wall. "You talk of the G's, huh? To me! *Corpo di corpo!* for this I kill you where you stand. No, but I should waste ammunition that later may be handy for these G's. Did you think I'd be afraid of any Federal men? No, it is they who are afraid of me! Bah! For you, maybe this will teach you to talk to me of your lousy Federal men—!"

Old Anecdote had wanted to ask about a lot of things. Why the other men in the party had started stripping their coats, shirts, changing their clothes like volunteer firemen on a call. Why they'd bound Johnny Lane and left him in a corner behind a pile of Goodstone tires. Who the young girl was they'd brought in. But the fat man's blasphemous outburst left old Anecdote lockjawed with indignation, and the fat man never gave him a chance to speak.

Crack! Whipping upward with the Tommy gun, the fat man slashed the snubbed barrel across the side of old Anecdote's chin.

The gooseberry eyes glared down. "Tie up the old goat," he told Gum-boils. "Then look in that loft up there to see there ain't not gats or weapons about, This idiot, I leave him up there since no one would give one damn if we took him with us or not for hostage. Yes, the garage mechanic will serve for that. And slap some tape across this old fool's mouth. *Corpo!* I am to be threatened with the Federals by an idiot! For that perhaps we burn the garage when we go. That will teach him to talk to me of Feds. Who"—he glared at the man, Julius—"is this General Grant?"

OLD ANECDOTE wondered where he was. For what seemed a long time—the clock is slow for the old—he lay there in the stuffy dark, breathing heavily through his nose, blinking the pain from his eyelids, unable to rise because a huge hand seemed pressed across his mouth and his joints wouldn't work. A familiarity about his shadowed surroundings was reassuring, but somewhere something was wrong, everything had gone awry. His face ached; his wrists and ankles throbbed; his head felt as if it were on fire; yet his main feeling on waking had been one of red rage—rage against something—some insult—what?

Presently, moving his eyes, he saw the little front window; recognized his loft. He was lying on the floor beside the iron cot. The shoulder of a great yellow moon was framed in an upper corner of the window, like the Hallowe'en pumpkin some of the village boys had had once poked up there on a clothespole, and a streak of chrome splashed the inside wall under the eaves and touched with color the tarnished cord of an old blue cobwebby hat hanging there. His campaign hat!

Somehow sight of the hat brought a fresh upsurge of rage; he tried to open his mouth, couldn't move his jaws, lay back panting, miserable, confused. Voices under the floor, murmurous, guttural—Lem and the boys must be having a harangue—

no, Lem and the boys had gone to Brockton— He turned his head painfully and saw a cone of yellow light spearing up through a knothole in the floor.

"Did ya get it, Skull?" a voice was asking.

There came the sound of the sheet-iron garage door being shut, then a hoarse voice saying, "Sure, we got it. Dynamite didn't even have to blow the can. Crazy old safe you could've opened with a musical saw. Next door, that dairy place, the stuff was in a cash box yuh wouldn't leave a counterfeit dime in."

"I don't like it," a woman's voice said harshly. "Takin' time out to clean a crossroads like this for th' sake of carfare."

"Three hundred an' eight bucks," a basso voice said, "may come in handy, if we have to lay over a long time."

The greasy guttural voice said, "That all you got, Dynamite?"

"That's all, Boss. Most of it in that feed store. Not much, but I only hadda reach for it. Julius had the low down, all right, there ain't a farmer left in th' neighborhood. Only one old woman in that red farmhouse up the hill."

"And she's deaf an' blind," a voice explained. "It's like I told you, Chief. The whole county goes over to that Brockton field day."

"Yeah, but when do they come back?" the woman's voice asked.

"Not till after the torchlight parade and the barbecue," the first speaker declared. "I tell you, this is a hick burg, Toots. Three barns an' a church. They leave their doors open at night."

Vague memory struggled in old Anecdote's aching head. Toots! He'd heard that name before. Straining his ears, he kept his eyes on the lighted knothole.

The woman's voice, complaining, came up from below. "Well, I don't like it. Why do we wait here, instead of a cabin in the woods or—"

"*Corpo!*" said the guttural. "Must I explain fifty times? The field behind this cursed garage is the only one in these hills where the Duke could come over from Brockton an' land his plane ain't it?"

"Why ain't he here?"

"Keep your shirt on!" the guttural changed to a snarl. "He does that night-flyin' stunt over to the field day, see? That's his excuse for bringin' his plane up here. He couldn't just lam off without no alibi. They think he's goin' back to Newark after the show, but he cuts for here, lands in the dark, picks us up with the kid an' we scram for Canada."

"Suppose he don't come."

"My own brother? Huh! He knows. I would cut him up to spaghetti. But the job is soft. Soft as a dead puppy. By plane, Canada is ten minutes. Over the border, we drop off in parachutes when we get above that farm, and then we"—the voice blurred, came back—"hold the kid there with this garage mechanic here as hostage in case they get tough. The Duke flies back to Newark—in the night. Who knows anything?"

"But if they trail us?"

"They won't. Them *'Road Closed'* signs will keep off traffic, tonight anyhow. They're lookin' for a black sedan. We fill that with soup, run it into the bridge, blow up the car and bridge with it—they think we're in the river. Skull and Gum-boils pull out in Julius's car, doublin' back. Decoy 'em south, see? Got that extra carburetor fixed, Julius?"

"Ready to roll, Chief."

"It ain't that I'm melting," the woman's voice was sullen. "It's only—well, I ain't never had the heat put on me by the Feds."

The guttural voice cursed contemptuously.

Old Anecdote sat upright in the blue darkness, choking. Something was fastening his jaws; his hands, he suddenly realized, were bound behind his back; his feet were tied. He'd been shut up here in the loft like a shock of grain; and those strangers down below were holding Lem's garage with guns. Maybe Lem had told them to come there, maybe the village boys had told them to shut him up like this—guns or not, old Anecdote didn't care! That fat man wasn't going to talk about Grant like he had. Old Anecdote set his six teeth; began to twist and strain at his ropes. That fat varmint couldn't get away with it. Wasn't nobody around this village going to speak that way of the Federals! Not in front of a man who'd took Richmond!

ILLUSIONS were something Johnny Lane could understand. Long as he lived—and that particular evening he didn't think it was going to be very long—he'd never forget the tricks his eyes began to play him. First, the girl. They were lying together on the cement floor behind a stack of tires, her face not five inches away. Opening one pain-dazed eye, he thought he was looking at a front page photograph in a newspaper. Girl's face under big blurred headlines. Seen it somewhere before. Pale little face under blonde ringlets. Seemed to be asleep, something frightening about it, the headlines—

Johnny Lane opened both eyes, stared. His mind cried the name, "Mary Clementridge—! In Lem's Garage—! Then he heard, somewhere near, men's voices; saw shadows with guns trooping across candle light on the wall. He'd been working on an olive sedan—a black car had stopped at the gas pump—a fat man—*Joe Gravatti!* The thought strained sweat beads through the skin on his forehead. Mary Clementridge. The Gravatti Mob. Two hundred thousand dollars ransom—and the whole village over to Brockton!

Fainting is funny. Maybe you're out thirty seconds, maybe an hour. When he opened his eyes again, he suffered another shock. By turning his head a trifle, he could see through a peep hole in the tire stack. Seen from that perspective, in candle light, the garage was a shadow-peopled cavern, everything tilted and at queer angles. Walls and floor tipped, blurred, came back into ghostly focus; he saw a candle set on a work bench; a greenish-faced fat man sitting near in Lem's old Morris chair, a machine gun rifle across his knees. A woman in black stood beside the chair, lighting a cigar. A stunted man and a thin man paced back and forth the length of the closed garage doors, and another skinny man sat on the steps leading up to old Anec-dote's loft, rifle in the crotch of his arm. The city man who'd been stalled out front was bending over a suitcase; but when he straightened up, he had a beard and a mustache.

Johnny Lane heard him say, "How's that?" and the woman growled, "Well, I hope anyhow you'll take it off at night."

Johnny Lane knew they were waiting for someone, because the fat man kept looking at his watch. Another queer thing: All except two of the party were wearing short leather jackets and odd bundles like Boy Scout knapsacks were strapped to their backs. A choking fear gripped his throat. The girl lying against the wall wore one of these funny knapsacks too. He tried to ease his shoulders, and found they'd strapped one on him!

"See if the hick garage mechanic's woke up," the fat man said suddenly. "If he has, give him the needle like you give the girl. Not too much, or it'll croak him."

He saw the woman start across the floor, a shiny little tube in her fingers. He didn't know, then, whether he fainted or not; he seemed to hear the woman's growl: "Still out!" When he opened his eyes the third time, the illusion was stranger still. Someone was watching him!

Johnny Lane's scalp crawled. Someone was watching him, but it wasn't anyone in that repair room. Those gunmen were pacing around the floor like caged tigers, all except the thin man who sat on the loft steps, swearing, arguing together, paying him no attention. The girl beside him slept. Yet—the flesh pinched on Johnny Lane's neck—he could seventh-sense himself as the center of some secret gaze, some intent scrutiny, the same feeling he'd had up in the Maine woods when he'd turned around once and seen a bear—ready to pounce at him—

AN EYE! His startled gaze, drawn as if by hypnotism, looked up. Breath froze in his lungs. He could have sworn he'd seen it. Now there was nothing but a little black hole in the boards, a little black hole with wisps of smoke from the woman's cigar sucked up through on a draught from somewhere. No! There it was again. An eye! Pale blue, shiny as a marble, glittering and angry as the Eye of Jehovah, looking straight down at him from the ceiling. Even had his lips been untaped, Johnny Lane could have uttered no sound. He could see the eye gleaming fixedly down at him, then letting its awful gaze roam around the garage; focussing on the thin man who guarded the steps to the loft, settling finally in bright malevolence on the fat foreigner in the Morris chair. Johnny Lane lay ossified, hardly daring to breathe. He would not have been surprised to see the fat man vanish in a spiral of greasy smoke, like vaseline under the focus of a burning glass. The ferocity of that eye in the ceiling would have intimidated a tiger. They read the Bible in Four Corners, and Johnny Lane had never been quite as frightened in his life.

A shiver galloped through him.

Sweat clouded his own vision; when he once more dared to open his lids, the eye had gone. He'd dreamed it then. If only he was dreaming the rest of this! No, those voices, the scuffle of pacing shoes, the smell of cigar smoke, the glimpse of faces and guns seen through chinks in the tire stack—all that was only too real. This girl lying here asleep—twelve years old, the papers had said—how strangely quiet she was—her small face wan and colorless—her mud-spattered dress—not at all like a Boston heiress hunted for by all the police of New England. In mounting panic he wondered if she was dead. But she was breathing, he saw. Faintly. Irregularly. The way sick people breathe.

The fat man's voice come to his ears. "Okay, Dynamite, it's your move."

The short man's basso answered. "Time to blast th' bridge?"

"The Duke oughta be flyin' over here in twenty minutes. He's puttin' on his air show now. Be sure there's enough nitro to blow up that bridge, see? Steer the car straight for the bridge-head and run like hell. I want plenty of soup in that sedan, so by the time they dredge all th' pieces of junk outa the river and find we ain't in the car, we'll be already three weeks in Canada. Catch on?"

"There's enough soup in that car to lift Brooklyn Bridge."

"Then make it snappy. I don't wanta give no early sleepers a chance t' get back here from Brockton before we take off. Th' explosion is Duke's signal to come. With that bridge gone, there can't nobody reach the village from that direction without goin' a thirty mile detour to cross th' river. An' they won't be comin' from the east, since we blocked t' road."

Sickness squashed Johnny Lane's chest where his heart had been. If they blew up that bridge, no-one could reach the village from Brockton way for hours. And they had the east road blocked. They were taking an airplane—

"Be in Canada in no time," the fat man was saying. "Never find us there. An' get back here quick, Dynamite, I wantcha to fire this garage. We're burning her up when we leave, an' that old man up there'll learn to hold his gabby tongue."

Stiff in terror, Johnny Lane saw the short man open the sheet-iron door a foot; squeeze out into the moonlight. His dark face grinned back through the opening, "I won't be five minutes, Boss. Listen for the smack." The door closed stealthily. Johnny Lane moaned soundlessly; began a desperate struggling at his bonds. Ropes binding his wrists behind his back might have been made of steel. His shoes couldn't budge.

His numbed mind was repeating, "They're flying the girl to Canada, an' me with her. They're going to blow up the bridge an' come back an' burn up old Anecdote alive. Oh, God, don't let them do it—don't let them do it!"

It was not until some minutes later that he realized nothing had happened. Or—to put it the other way around—something had!

WATCH in hand, rocking slowly, the fat man was swearing in thick, sulphurous Sicilian, glaring at the dial as if *it* were at fault. On the steps to the loft, Gum-boils shifted his seat uneasily. Julius was petting his beard and staring at the floor; Toots sauntered up and down, chewing her cigar and rubbing her elbows.

She halted abruptly and snapped out, "Has anybody *heard* anything?"

Julius looked up startled. "Not a thing."

"I tell you," the one called Skull took his ear away from the front door, and turned his head to drawl, "I didn't even hear him start th' car. We had it parked alongside the feed store across th' way, pointed toward th' bridge for a quick take-off."

"Can't you see it from here, if you open them doors a crack?"

"Nah. Gas pump and that chestnut tree cuts off the view. Can't see out to the road from here."

"You keep opening those doors," the fat man warned viciously, "an' some punk motorist the other side the valley will see our lights an' start comin' acrost the bridge for gas. We can't blow up everybody we—"

"From all th' noise around here," the woman growled, "we can't even seem to blow up a bridge. Or am I going deaf? I ain't heard a sound out there since Dynamite left."

"He's had time enough," Gum-boils put in, "to blow up Sing Sing!"

Skull's forehead worried, "I didn't even hear him start the—"

The fat man sprang up ragefully. *"Madonna!* Are you trying to give me the jitters? Dynamite can't start the sedan. Julius, you tear your pants goin' across that road an' find out what's wrong. The Duke can't loop the loop all night, waitin' for that signal."

It was quiet in the garage after Julius left. Nobody moved. Tense, his pores dripping icewater, Johnny Lane lay helpless on the floor behind the tire stack staring at the ceiling where a moment ago he was sure there'd been an eye. It wasn't there now. It had vanished the moment that man Julius had started to open the doors.

Johnny Lane moaned in thought, "I'm dreaming—it's all a horrible dream." It was like a nightmare, too, this waiting and waiting—and nothing happening. Ears aching at the strain, Johnny listened for the crash that would cut him off from all help—his face screwed up as if he was watching someone blow more and more air in a balloon—the silence deepened.

Then, little by little—he knew he wasn't dreaming this—the silence was disturbed. First, the creak of rockers under the Morris chair, squeaking faster and faster. Then the scuff of the woman's high heels pacing up and down.

"Boss, I ain't heard a thing yet," the man on the loft steps said plaintively.

Moving his head to peep, Johnny Lane saw the fat man's face going purple. The little gooseberry eyes were glittering, and the forehead seemed to sizzle. The fat man pocketed his timepiece and sprang up suddenly, gripping that Tommy gun as if he wanted to shoot somebody. "Who can hear anything," he screamed at the woman, "with *you* tramping up and down the room? Sit down! Sit down, do you hear?"

She whirled, snatching out the cigar. "Tell me why he don't come back! Why ain't either of them come back? They've taken a run-out powder, that's why! I could be across that road an' back in half a minute an'—"

"Then get across it," the gooseberry eyes gave a knife-thrust stare. "Maybe they're tryin' to start the car. Maybe they're playin' dice. Whatever it is, tell 'em I want that bridge blown out in three minutes, or I'll be over there an' shoot them into strawberry jam! Get out," he screamed at the woman, "an' be back here in just one minute. Don't stay. I wanta know why the stall. I'll knock you dead if you ain't back here in just one minute!"

CHAPTER III

NOTHING HAPPENED. THE woman had a revolver in her hand as she went out. Skull closed the door behind her; leaned there loosely, staring down at his grounded rifle. Gum-boils shifted on the steps; spat. The fat man folded his hands across his stomach as if he was afraid someone might steal it, and leaned back, his eyes narrowed at the doors, Tommy gun balanced across his knees. Stiff on the floor, Johnny Lane was staring in mounting terror at the ceiling where he was certain, for a third time, he'd seen the eye.

But it was gone again—there was no sound anywhere—presently the rockers were going under the fat man's chair. Suddenly the man on the loft steps blurted:

"I'd think them guys was knocked off, but we'd 'a' heard the shots."

"There ain't been a sound out there," Skull turned from the doors to whisper. Sweat twinkled all over his face as he whispered. "Chief, you don't think the G's—"

"No!"

"Then they've ditched us. Lammed. Left us holding the bag."

"The woman," came the guttural snarl, "she's late. It's your job, Gum-boils."

"Boss," the thin man on the steps said huskily, "dontcha think Skull better go with me?"

"There's too many out there now."

"But, Chief—!"

The fat man whipped to his feet. Panted: "Go out there! Kill her! Find out what's happened to Dynamite and Julius! Come back!"

Yellow-green pallor crawled up Gum-boils' jawbones. He stood up shakily, rifle in elbow. His eyes, shaded by a cap brim, moved from side to side. He said in a queer, coughing way, "I know. It's a trap. You've got one of the boys planted out there with a knife. You greasy slob, you're one by one tryin' to knock us off." The man's eyes began to cry. "I know you, Joe. You wanta keep the snatch for yourself, an' you're tryin' to knock us off!" The thin man shook there on the loft steps, coughing and crying.

In the fat man's hands the Tommy gun jerked and smoked. *Dud-dud-dud-dud!* Arms flying out, legs doing the splits, the thin man seemed to splatter all over the steps. The fat man sat down in the Morris chair, and said, "I'll make some noise around here!" looking at Skull.

Skull eyed the red heap on the steps dreamily. Smoke dissolved in flitting candle light and silence. Skull rubbed a wet cheekbone with an elbow and murmured, "Maybe that'll bring 'em back."

They waited. "Okay, Chief," the man at the doors said after a minute, "I'll go. Only I wish I knew what was out there."

The fat man whispered, "Dynamite goes an' don't come back. Julius goes to find Dynamite, an' don't come back. That dame goes to find the first two, an' don't come back—!" He was on his feet, face-flesh twitching, pig-eyes flickering between slitted lids. "What is this? I'd think it was the Feds, only they'd be in *here* by now. *Corpo!* are they trying to cross Joe Gravatti? Skull, you stick by me and I'll split the ransom. You find out where those rats have gone, and I'll split with you!"

"Can I have a bronze coffin like you gave Mugs O'Flannigan, Chief?"

"You've gotta come back," was the guttural whisper. "You can't leave me here alone. I've give you more than one break, Skull. *Maria!* if you lam on me, I'm cooked. We still got a chance. Open them doors. I'll watch you as far as the road. If they get you, they get me, too. Let's go!"

Johnny. Lane could see it all. The red mess on the loft steps. The fat man mushroomed down beside the Morris chair, clutching the Tommy gun. The one called Skull shoving open, inch by inch, the sheet-iron doors. Moonlight slanted in through the widening entry-way; outside there was a silver-etched picture of the driveway and Mocony pump, the chestnut tree beyond—silence and no one there.

Then Skull was outside, a running shadow, crossing the open gravel in five quick bounds, stooped low and leaping zigzag so as not to be caught from behind. But it wasn't the fat man's Tommy gun that stopped him. Johnny Lane would never forget that as long as he lived. The way Skull fled past the chestnut tree, stopped up short in his tracks, jumped back, whirled with a yell.

"Chief! They're out there in the—*Ow!*"

There wasn't a shot. As far as Johnny Lane's terrified glimpse could see, there wasn't anything. Skull dropped his rifle, put hands to face and stumbled forward, fell as if dead in the moon-washed driveway.

Johnny Lane would never forget what happened after that, either. How the fat man swore. Spun around. Sprang straight for the corner where the boy lay helpless beside the unconscious little girl.

Then he bent down—only it was more of a swoop, quick and savage and hateful—and struck in at them with his hands spread to grab.

The feel of those sweaty squat arms clutching him up, dragging him across the floor, would curdle Johnny's blood for many a day. The sewerish puffs of garlic breath in his face. The way, hugged against the fat man's chest, he was rushed to the door and impelled out into the moonlight as a shield. His adhesive-taped mouth made the soundless shrieks of nightmare, and his strength turned to water in the Sicilian's savage grip. Johnny could not so much as squirm.

They might have reached the olive sedan the other side of the Mocony pump, if the fat man hadn't stopped that split second to see what was out there in the road. Three bodies lined up on the moon-yellowed concrete like corpses after battle—Dynamite, Julius and Toots, three in a row; and Skull stretched out in similar pose under the chestnut tree. Involuntarily the fat man halted, rolled his little eyes in terror at the night; gasped, *"Madonna!"* and shifted his grip on the Tommy gun. Johnny Lane's stomach was a stone going down for the last time. There was, in the night out there, no sign of what had felled those four—no sign of anything.

Then, *ping!*

TO JOHNNY LANE it sounded like an invisible banjo string snapping in mid air. Something flashed in moonlight across his line of vision, and the rear window smashed in the olive sedan. It hadn't come from the direction of the road. Overhead, in the moony night above them, there was a shrill and spectral cry.

"Missed!"

Whirled about-face in his captor's grip, Johnny Lane felt his eyes and hair go up at the same time.

Framed in the little window of the loft above the garage—in moonshine as dim and faded as a time-bleached oil painting— a ghost! The ghost of a Civil War veteran in tarnished brass buttons and moth-eaten blue—a face of shriveled parchment under the fragments of a campaign hat, acorns bobbing on frayed cord, gold threads peeling from the shoulder tabs—por- trait of one of the Boys in Blue painted in moonbeams and cobweb; a mirage from the dust blown off a history book— something a mere breath of wind would whisk away. Only the eyes were alive. Squirrel-bright pins of cobalt—two fierce old lights in the shriveled parchmenty face.

Johnny's throat screamed, "Anecdote!" as he recognized the eye.

He was a little surprised and a good deal relieved to dis- cover that it hadn't been Jehovah after all.

The fat man squalled up. "It's the idiot!"

"Learn ye an' all y're dirty kind to laugh at us Federals!" came shrilling from the phantom face. "Goin' to burn up th' soldier who took Richmond, was ye? Thought a man as knew Gen'ral Grant would turn an' run from yer new-fangled shootin' irons? I'll learn ye su'thin about us Yankee Federals—!"

Johnny Lane saw it all. He saw the head come out of that lofted window in the garage front like a cuckoo popping out of a clock. He saw a whittled forked stick in the old man's knotty fist; saw him cock back his left arm as one pulls a bow and arrow; saw that blazing, tiger-fierce eyeball squinting aim through the forked stick's *Y.*

Ping!

Metal whistled overhead as the fat man hurled himself and Johnny Lane to the gravel. The olive sedan's spare tire whammed like an exploding shell. Corkscrewed on the ground, Johnny saw the Tommy gun jerking and smoking in the fat man's sausage-like hands—*dud-dud-dud-dud!* The head had popped back into that upper window like a crazy cuckoo clock striking one.

Johnny ground his cheek in the driveway as the fat man knelt over him and cleaned the little window above with fusillade after fusillade, riddling the sill, peppering the clapboards underneath, cutting chunks from the roofline. Splinters flew and scattered; a tin drain pipe fell; a shutter came crashing down. Impossible for any living target to have survived such a machine-gunning, but the gunman's blast was answered by a yell from the loft, an eerie battle whoop that drowned the bombardment echoes with defiance, and wrung from the Sicilian's neck a raging squall.

"*Corpo di Corpo!*"

The man's bull voice rose, and hung trembling in the air.

Gun hugged to belly, the fat man went for the garage door like a swollen ferret for a squirrel's nest, shoes beating across the ground like little hoofs. Johnny Lane never knew what came over him. Somehow he was no longer afraid. All he knew was that he had to stop that murderer before he reached the loft up there. Bound, gagged, helpless though he was, the boy rolled and twisted and dragged himself in clumsy pursuit; and got there in time to see the end.

In time to see the fat man start up that steep flight of steps. In time to see the trap fly open at the top and old Anecdote standing there in the dimness, his boots braced across the opening, knees bent, weapon aimed, and under the brim of the old slouch hat that brilliant and ferocious eye glaring down.

"Halt, in th' name o' the Republic!"

So the Armies of the North might have cried down at Rebellion. So Thomas might have stood at Chickamauga or Meade at Gettysburg or Grant against Disunion. Or David might have stood so, confronting Goliath. Only David wasn't ninety and facing a Thompson machine gun.

On the other hand, Goliath didn't have to run up wet steps. The fat man slipped on Gum-boils; fell upstairs. Old Anecdote charged down, shouting. Collision! The Tommy gun firing every which way. Smoke, livid flame-bursts, Sicilian oaths and Yankee battle cry, old soldier and gangster and dead man coming down all in a heap.

For a moment, the three bodies all interlocked in a writhing, twisted tangle, like one of those rolling, cyclone-formed mêlées that movie cartoonists denote by a swirl of lines with asterisks and exclamation points shooting out of them at impossible angles.

Johnny Lane got into it somehow, arching his trussed shoulders and kicking with locked feet. The fat man, tangled with dead man, bound man and history, went somersaulting on the floor. Johnny jammed his legs between the fat man's knees and tackled him flat. But such reinforcements didn't count. It was the old man's fight after all.

Old Anecdote stood upright on the bottom step, arm cocked, eyeball blazing through the forked stick's Y, at the moment the fat man gained his feet not a jump away. Looking up from the floor, Johnny saw the Tommy gun squirt a burst of flame; simultaneously something metallic whizzed *zing!* through his line of vision. Old Anecdote's wail was echoed as he fell. The fat man's face might have caught a thunderbolt. Blood flashed from the socket where a gooseberry eye had been; in a splash of scarlet the body squatted down.

When the smoke and terror cleared away, Johnny Lane lay crying by himself. Far across the valley the echoes of the Tommy gun were clattering, and on the road the other side of the river droned the sound of a car coming fast.

OLD ANECDOTE, when they reached him, was still alive. Andrew Dobbs, despite the stains on his brand new uniform, put an arm around the pinched old shoulders to ease them up; and Lem's hands were gently hunting the asked-for chaw of tobacco; while Charlie Rambow and the others stood there silently weeping—

"Grant says, 'Jonesey,' he says, puttin' his hand right on my shoulder, 'Jonesey,' he says, 'you gotta hold that hill. You hold that hill an' don't let the Rebels get through, an' it's just like you took Richmond all by yourself,' he says—"

"Sure, Anecdote. Sure!"

"I was up there alone, y'see? Marooned-like. Outa bullets. No reinforcements. Them Rebels come up again, but I held 'em off—"

"You sure did, soldier. All by yourself and out of bullets, too."

The old man opened his eyes and gazed in cloudy apprehension at the faces looking down. "Dontcha wanta know *how* I held 'em off—*how*—?"

"Don't make no difference, soldier. We believe you. We sure do."

They stood there, shifting on their feet, clearing their throats, looking down at him and not knowing what to say to him at all.

The dimming eyes wandered in vague bewilderment; fixed suddenly on something lying on the garage floor; kindled and cleared and shone in happy triumph.

"Why, o' course!" the voice was jubilant, piping strong. "That's how I held off them Johnny Rebs that night. When I was alone an' outa bullets, an' seen 'em a-comin' up th' hill. That's how I held 'em off. With *that!*"

At first appearance the whittled forked stick, lying there in a scatter of ring-bolts, rusty nuts and scrap-bits, meant nothing. Johnny Lane had to show them the long strip of inner tube that was fastened to the prongs of the stick.

"That's how I took Richmond," the old man was whispering. "Yessir, that's how I done it. Clumb a tree, when I saw them

Rebs was a-comin', an' made me one of those! That's how I held that hill. With a sling-shot—!"

Afterwards, Mule Lickett said in a voice of awe, "They do say they're awful strong—"

But Andrew Dobbs thought the real miracle was the old man's getting loose to begin with. Human strength of any power couldn't have broken those ropes like that. You could see the parted strands of hemp on old Anecdote's ankles and wrists.

It wasn't until the State Police got there to pick up the gangsters who'd only been knocked unconscious, to revive the little Clementridge girl and send her to the hospital, to dispatch an officer to arrest the Duke, and to clean up the mess—it wasn't until they examined Joe Gfavatti's fat corpse that Four Corners learned the answer. A rusty piece of file—discarded by Lem to the old man's junk heap in the loft—must have cut the old man's bonds before it had been slung-shot like a thunderbolt into the fat man's gooseberry eye.

FOUR CORNERS may not be as big as New York, but it has as much civic pride. Take the Decoration Day parade, and the whole town turns out—I mean, the *whole* town. There's the Protective Volunteer Fire Company, the Girl Scouts, the children from District School Number Nine, and two hay wagons loaded with geraniums. Led by the boys of the Legion—Bowd Post—Mule Lickett, Andrew Dobbs and the others—all looking pretty fine in their new uniforms, and Charlie Rambow showing them how it's done on a snare drum. March? They come across the river bridge with more flags flying than you'd expect, and they march right up to a halt between Clapp's Feed Store and Lem's Garage, and stand at attention before the monument.

No, Four Corners may not be very big, but they'll tell you that monument is as fine a piece of Vermont marble as ever was erected anywhere. Right beside the highway it stands, where the traffic can't help but see it, a tall white cenotaph of simple stateliness, simply inscribed.

He Took Richmond

If you ask the folks around Four Corners about it, they'll surprise you by talking about the Mary Clementridge kidnaping—remember?—and the old man who, single-handed, captured the Gravatti gang. Ask about Richmond and you'll get a cold Yankee stare and perhaps sharp advice to go read your history. That's what they told me when I first moved there, and I pored over the village records a long musty time before I found any reference to the old soldier in question. Then it had little to do with the Civil War.

He'd been turned down at the recruiting bureau in 1861 because, on applying for enlistment, he'd told the officers how—single-handed and out of bullets, I'll warrant—he'd held off the British for one whole night—and won the Battle of Lexington!

II

FRIVOLOUS SAL

The last testament of a hayseed Cleopatra.

CHAPTER I

FRIVOLOUS SAL WAS dying.

What happened on the eve of her death took place about the time the Black Legion was dirtying up the headlines, and this story is dedicated to all such underhand clans, to all witch-burners and lynchers everywhere, to those who would crucify a brother for the color of his skin or the size of his nose, to the Pharisees ready to launch the first stone at another's mistakes.

There's a bit of the Judge in all of us, so it's not surprising this should come to the surface in a place as narrow as Four Corners. Not that country towns are the only strongholds of violent bigotry (our world capitols have their whipping-posts today) but you hear of it more readily in a country town. An explosion, for the quiet of the hills, is louder.

And the hills around Four Corners are pretty quiet. News, when there is any, travels fast and echoes farther. Death in a rural community is pretty big news, especially if it happens to be overtaking one of the county's oldest citizens. Villagers consult down at the Feed Store; neighbors run in and out; Theodore Seymore, undertaker, perches like a gaunt black buzzard in his parlor window, waiting with fishy talons spread to catch the prize; there's a lot of head-shaking and loud talk. But this time the talk was low, it was the echoes that were loud.

"Yes, sir." Ear against palm, Mule Lickette, leaning on the Mocony pump in front of Lem's Garage, fixed a somber gaze on the twilight-shadowed ridge the other side of Blue Valley.

"Yes, sir, I reckon her number's up this time. Doc Trosch was there again las' night. Lungs. Gets 'em in the end, every time."

"She ain't been seen by nobody 'cept th' Doc come five years, now," Lawyer Bickle averred, scratching the side of his beaked nose with a barley straw. "Don't suppose she sees *him* very often, way he charges."

"Dunna how she's kep' alive since McGuire foreclosed th' mortgage on that road place of her'n," somebody said. "How she lives on alone in that shack up there beats me. Never comin' out ner seein' nobody."

"Wouldn'ta heard she was dyin' if Postmaster Crackenbush hadn't seen th' flag up on her letter box where she'd left a note for th' Doc."

Mule Lickette stared across the valley. "Funny, ain't it. A woman hermit."

"Yeah, after you remember—" a voice from in back broke off.

"Can't carry on the way she useta an' get away with it," Leonidas Barrows pronounced sternly. "Dyin', is she? Well—"

THERE was a book behind that grim-voiced "Well—", and I thought I knew which book it was. *Proverbs*, perhaps, or one of the Prophets. *Isaiah*. "Cast thy bread upon the waters—" Four Corners may have hung on to their Testaments longer than your finger-snapping urban locales, which is true of most communities that must work with their hands. You see stone fences around Four Corners and those fences came out of the soil. People who farm such fields—especially the oldsters who did it by arm-power—know the truth of *As ye sow, so shall ye reap.*

There was a number of the older generation in the evening's gathering before Lem's—their wives at a knitting social at Grange Hall—and I took it from their expressions that the person in discussion (who was not at the knitting social) had sown neither wisely nor well. A woman hermit. I was intrigued. In residence only a year, and therefore a stranger, in Four Corners I had to ask about her.

Leonidas Barrows, who is the County Bank, answered with

a sound *humph*, indicating the subject unworthy of my investigation. A general drawing-in of chins from the other oldsters there—Horace Johns, head of the Dairyman's League; Mordecai Sailor, owner of Blue Valley Farms; Town-Clerk Tinney, Lawyer Bickle and some others. Not one of that group drives a car above a Buick; there's more money among them than you'll find in many a fleet of V-16s on Park Avenue, and twice the pride.

It remained for the younger generation (in their liberal

forties) to tell me about the woman reported as dying. Her time, so far as I could gather, had been the Gay Nineties when people were humming waltzes, looking at Gibson Girls and whispering of Suffragets. Not country people, though; leastwise, not around Four Corners. Young unmarried ladies—self respecting ones—wore hair ribbons at twenty-five, spent Sundays cooking Sunday dinner for Pa, and, around Four Corners, knew how to get milk out of a cow. But around Four Corners, same as anywhere a girl ought to've married by twenty-five. Hadn't ought to have uppity notions about travel and dancing and sending 'way to Albany after hats and such, even if her father did own one of the best farms in the valley.

Her father wanted her to marry and settle down, but she hadn't. Even at twenty she was always talking about fashions and trips to places and learning to waltz. You know the kind of girl. Flighty. All the village boys courtin' her, but she didn't want to be a farmer's wife. Too good for everybody. Pity, too, for her father was elder in the church.

Then it looked like she was going to settle down—her father let on she was engaged to a mighty-fine catch, but it was to be a secret till the wedding, and she'd run off to Boston; yes, sir, run off all by herself. And that just broke the old man's heart. He up and shot himself next night out in the barn; committed suicide, he felt that bad.

Scandal? There'd 've been a scandal anywhere. Whole valley knew she'd run away from her wedding; never learned who'd been jilted, whoever it was, he'd been decent enough to keep his mouth shut. Rumored it was a local boy, but maybe it was someone at Brockton. Anyhow, she'd inherited her father's farm by his death, and on top of that she'd had the gall to come back to Four Corners all rigged out in mourning clothes from one of the smart shops in Boston, and when she got off the local at the depot she hadn't shed a tear. Not one. Nor said she was sorry, nor nothin'. And it was just the same, folks said, as if she'd killed her own father.

They still talked about the funeral. Her sitting there dry-eyed without any kind of expression on her face. Deacon Wine-garth—he'd been alive then—preaching the funeral sermon and working in the line about "a serpent's tooth and a thankless child." But she hadn't batted a dry eye. Nobody ever saw her cry even once.

AFTER that the whole valley cut her dead. You could hardly blame them. Wasn't she out of mourning in a month, wearing a bunch of new frocks, city clothes bought with her father's hard-earned money? Coming into the post office, looking neither right nor left and sending off letters here for a piano, and there for all kinds of furniture? But it was the automobile that finished her. One of those get-out-and-get-under kind, bright red. It came from Albany and she drove it herself with the top down. Talk about brass!

Wasn't a woman in the valley who'd speak to her after that, and it just seemed like she was trying to flaunt her brazenness at the whole county. She planted shrubs around the farm and sodded the lawn for croquet. She used to bat the balls around all day Sunday by herself, and the minister went up to speak to her about it and she told him to please stay away. You could imagine the farm didn't last long, run like that.

Four Corners learned she'd had to mortgage it over in Brockton, heavily. Had to sell the lower fifty to meet the payment. It didn't stop her, though. She went to Albany for a visit, and come back letting on she was going to marry a city man. There wasn't any holding her, then; you'd see a city crowd up for weekend parties, singing and shouting ill over the place—until the one she'd got engaged to went joy-riding down the valley one night in that red car and smashed plumb into a train. Killed dead as stone. That quieted her down for a spell.

She was at it again, though, in about two years—there were stories she'd been seen over at Brockton with some of the boys around town. Then she went to Chicago for a year selling another piece of the farm to go, and when she sold the woods she went to New York. Plain wild. Somebody saw her at a party in a New York Hotel, drinking champagne. A man was kissing her right at the table, and everybody was laughing and carrying on. That was the day before War was declared—afterwards Four Corners read in the paper she'd been married to an army captain. Nobody ever heard a word about him afterwards 'till, a month after the Armistice, she was back in Four Corners selling more of the farm. Seemed she'd just been divorced and was out of money. Had spent a fortune gallivanting, and, as everybody knew she would, by winter that year she'd lost the whole farm.

It was quite a slide from there to the roadhouse on the state highway to Brockton, but the process of dissolution is as inevitable around Four Corners as anywhere. *As ye sow…* The roadhouse must have started with soft drinks, and gone hard. Prohibition—the old economics of supply and demand. The woman had to live.

It must have been a dingy place, but it brought echoes from the big towns and strangers whistling dance music. Mill workers from Brockton out for a Saturday night. Sneak in the back door for a brandy. It brought, too, an Irish bootlegger named Rion, red-haired and genial, who remained as husband and half-owner of this speakeasy, who put in a dice table, imported taxi dancers—you know how it would go. A Gambling Hell, Brockton pulpits called it; the Saratoga crowd went there. The pulpit in Four Corners called it worse. If you were bored with tilling rocky fields and your wife had gone to Cousin Hat's at Valley Spring and you wanted an evening out—

Somebody had to be shot there. Somebody was. Rion, in a dim room with the blinds down, in the back. He lived long enough to return the compliment, so there was nobody for the Law to make a lesson of but the proprietress who got, for violating the Eighteenth Ammendment, six years Federal Prison.

Even after that she had the brass to come back and try to open a roadside soft-drink stand across the valley. A citizen's committee, thinking of young sons just in highschool, took care of that. So she'd gone to live as a hermit on the last bit of property left her by her father, a shack in the woods. Nobody went there, unless it was a delegation of small boys to throw stones on Hallowe'en, and for five years she'd never come out. If she wanted anything, she left a note for the grocer in her letter box. The grocer would leave a package and pick up the coins. And for the last two winters the grocer had said it was hardly worth going across the valley after, maybe, once a week a pound of tea, box of crackers or something. Doc Trosch was the last man from Four Corners who'd seen her, and the undertaker would likely be next.

CHAPTER II

THIS MUCH I reconstructed from such laconic bits as, "Two marriages, a divorce, six years in Federal jail for runnin' one them places with the blinds down."—"Hard? Plain broke her father's heart."—"Recollect th' time she came back all painted up with lipstick; first I'd seen."—" 'Member seein' her whoopin' downhill in that red car, roarin' through th' village an' never bringin' her chin down an inch."—"Wonder what she looks like now?"—"Locked up in there like a hermit."

In the fading lilac of twilight I could just make out the gray roof of a shanty lonely on the pine ridge across the valley miles. Tiny in a desolation of timber. For contrast I was shown a meadowed reach along the river, white fences and barns that had once been her farm.

Mule Lickette shook his head. "The story of that woman's life would sure make a book."

Sheriff Vickers, from a back bench among the oldsters advised sourly, "You can read a couple chapters, if you're a mind, in th' records over at th' county jail."

"I wonder," from Cecil Price, a dairyman from over Brockton way, "I wonder, now, could she be writin' one?"

"Writin' a what, Ceace?"

"Writin' a book or suthin'. Y'know I drive by that shack four o'clock every mornin' to meet th' milk train. Well, since last winter, every mornin', I been seein' a light. Shutters closed on her winder, but I see a shadow there. She's sittin' up. So one mornin' I creep up for a look, an' make out a pen in her hand. Sure enough she's writin', I can see that much through the chinks. Got nobody to write letters to, so it must be a book."

"Say," Mule wondered, "maybe she's doin' th' story of her life."

"Maybe she's keepin a diary." It remained for Charlie Rambow to put the fuse that was later to touch off the explosion. Charlie's the village wit, and sometimes there are barbs to his jest. At the time there was a piquant edge to his smile, I thought, and a malice to his eye.

One of the older men didn't get it. "Her? A *dairy?*"

"*Dairies* is what you fellas around here keep," Charlie's grin twisted up. "Women keep *di*-aries. You know. Day to day accounts of everything happens in their lives."

I can recall (although I paid it no attention then) an arresting of side-conversation, a leaning forward of tilted chairs, one or two throat-clearings. Charlie enlarged with a flippant hand-wave, "They start writin''em when they're girls in school an' keep 'em through to the day they die. All their secret loves an' whatnot. Newspapers are always printing them by murderesses an' actresses an' such. Plenty musta happened in *her* life, she hasta stay up all night writin' it. Probably wants to bring it up to date 'fore she dies. Some record *she'd* leave behind—! Sure, I bet that's it. She's keepin' a *di*-ary!"

Silence spread in growing darkness. I could see a pin-point of yellow, now, marking the hermitage on that distant ridge. A figure that had been standing as a soundless shadow on the fringe of our forum, spoke out suddenly in a cutting tone. I recognized the acid voice of Doc Trosch. Afterwards I learned this saturnine old country doctor so far as his patients were concerned usually kept his mouth shut tight as a clam. At the moment I couldn't understand the razor in his tone or realize the aim of his scorn.

"Yes I've seen her writing in it. She *is* keeping a diary."

He snapped about-face on heel and walked away.

Women's voices were sauntering down the road from the direction of Grange Hall, and the men, who had been waiting for their wives, stood up. I walked toward the post office with Mule Lickette. "Guess she was pretty wild," he told me. "Good looker, too. Remember when I was a kid the flossy hats she wore, an' bright paint. 1912. My mom useta yank me into th' house, she go by."

"What was her name?"

"*Was*," he emphasized the past tense, "Clariselle Alders. Ain't heard it in thirty years though. We called her after a song she use to sing." He chuckled. "Frivolous Sal."

Neither of us knew the quiet that settled across the valley was the lull before the storm.

I DIDN'T mean to pry. I always take my daily walk across the bridge, following the river trail north from Peterson's Mill for solitude and escape from traffic. There's a scarecrow on a hillside over there I like to argue with, and often I take a fly rod for a try at rout. I had my rod that day. My friend Lion (you've seen his syndicated column) was coming up in a couple of weeks for fishing, and I wanted to test the pools.

But the fish weren't good sports that afternoon, and the scarecrow was uncommunicative. I sat down beside him in the blue-gold stillness, communing with a pipe. Presently my thoughts were drifting with the smoke uphill in the direction of a roof I could make out on the timber-lined ridge. Last light's story of human frailty, the fall from grace of another spirit, had left me in a grayish mood. I thought of the girl who'd sold her birthright for a pile of Albany hats: the price of plumes—a six years' prison sentence and a hermitage. A woman hermit. Prison could have been nothing to these last five years in "solitary," jailed in by the tight lips and averted eyes of her neighbors, committed to banishment by outraged society, exiled by a community's condemnation.

I thought of her dying alone under that roof up there. Surely she was paying now for her undaughterly "carryings-on," her father's suicide, her heartless adventuring. How expensive that unremorseful red car, the trips to Broadway, the broken conventions must seem. Or had the sordid roadhouse period ending in prison's gray left her encysted in a sullen vacuum from which all repentance had gone—a demented slattern jeering at all reproach. Likely; yet it didn't seem to fit with those nightly vigils at writing. That seemed queer.

From Clariselle Alders to Frivolous Sal—I confess it spoiled the fragrant perfection of that country afternoon—heaven help the person ostracized by a country town. Yet I wasn't the one to deny the implication of Leonidas Barrows that she had got her just desserts, or feel that she wasn't entitled to what the village dialect called her "comeuppance." There was a Law laid down long ago, *He that seeketh his life shall lose it—*

So I found my boots drifting with my thoughts toward the ridge. There's a fascination about a "death house"; my subconscious mind was already framing a novel around this human story, and I suppose I was impelled by a hunter's instinct after "material." Might pick up some authentic color around the place. We writers are coldblooded like that.

The ridge topped a slope known as Blueberry Hill; I found a path through the climbing acres of briar and mounted slowly, scaring chipmunks out of the weeds with the ferrule of my stick. Perspectives in open country are deceiving; it was a longer climb to the wooded ridge than I'd thought. And lonelier. The path was so little used there were places where it was choked with scrub, and when you rout out a couple of foxes you know you're pretty close to wilderness.

Afternoon was waning when I finally gained the ridge and came to the wood-hemmed wagon track down which Cecil Price made his morning drive with the milk. I saw the bones of some old farm machinery half buried in underbrush where starvation soil had killed enterprise; farther along the timber thickened into forest. I picked up the "color" of the place, all right. A dispiriting twilight lurked under the pines, and it was lonesome blue when I reached my objective. The shack could not have been more gloomy.

It stood in a stump-pegged clearing where someone had made a doomed attempt to pioneer a farm; I shouldn't have noticed it but for the rusty letterbox at roadside. The path up to the clearing was screened with undergrowth; the clapboard house, sagging in decay, darkly overshadowed by pines. There wasn't a sign of life about the place. Everything had run to seed. I could make out a ruptured sofa, disemboweled of its springs, on the rickety veranda. Windows with shutters closed, warped at crazy angles. A pile of old tin cans at one side; weeds closing in.

CHAPTER III

CERTAINLY NO WOMAN could be marooned in that squalid abode. I decided I'd found an abandoned shanty. Working my way around to the back, I came on the white skeleton of a dead horse, and sidestepping that, almost fell through the rotted timbering of a trap door covering a cistern. I had made up my mind this couldn't be the lair of anyone living or dying, when I heard from within that ruin a frail, phantasmal coughing—a wheezy thin whooping that might have been cut from a ghost's throat with a hack-saw. There was a torture in it worse than croup. I never heard a sound so moribund; for a moment I stood sick at the thing. There followed a sort of thumping sound at the shanty's front; I thought I heard feet shuffling in a front room, and in panic lest my spying be discovered, I ducked light foot away and into a nest of goldenrod. Looking back, I saw a shadow at the front door. The shadow of a man.

The twilight was almost gone and the man had appeared from nowhere with the silence of a secret. He was stooped like a thief in a cloak of darkness, hat low over his eyes, face dusk-blurred, his manner furtive as hide-and-seek. His knocking on the door was a clandestine summons—three knocks, then two—I recognized the thumping sound I'd heard, and I thought

I recognized the man. If he wasn't the Messenger from the Land of Shades come to collect his dead, I didn't know him.

"Sal," his voice was a low, haunting call intended for no farther than her door. "Sal—are you there?"

Actually my hair went up. It was the first time I'd heard anyone summoned to the grave—or heard the answer to *that* summons.

"Yes, I'm here," faint from behind the door. "Is that you—?" a croupy spasm of coughing; then weakly, "—is that you, Doctor Trosch?"

"No, Sal, it ain't. It's me—It's Ginger—"

The occult voice had changed to a whine, and I saw it once that an emissary from the Netherworld would hardly be named Ginger. Too, the nasal twang, local to the valley, sounded dimly familiar. But I could recall no "Ginger" around Four Corners, and apparently the name had been in desuetude for its owner, after a baited silence, repeated in a tone of plaintive petition, "Ginger! Don't you remember, Sal? Don't you remember Ginger—?"

"Yes, I do. *Go away!*"

Ordinarily I'm not in favor of eavesdropping, but the response from behind that door, the sudden fierce uplift of a feminine voice roused from a coughing whisper to that steely vitality, overwhelmed my manners. Altogether these circumstances were queer. The visitor's skulking appearance, the voice from within, the man's further appeal had me listening all ears.

"But I got to see you, Sal. Sal, please! Let me in!"

"You're too late. I don't want to see you. Go away!"

"Too late?" Tone of panic; then wheedling desperation. "Just let me in for a minute. Only a minute—! I want to do something for you, Sal. I can't tell you out here—"

"Go—" there was a gag of stifled coughing that ended in a command like knife-thrust through the door, "*away!*"

I don't know what was said then, for the man had his mouth at the key-hole, whining a low singsong, like an entreating dog's, but I heard the last part of it clearly enough. "A thousand dollars, Sal. Yes, I will—"

Fiercely low from behind the door, "No!"

"Fifteen hundred," the shadow at the door falsettoed. "I wouldn't do it, but, seeing it's you—fifteen hundred, Sal. All right—?"

The answer was an echo of laughter that came through those gray walls high and dry and thin, a laugh like the inkling of thread-strung needles, infinitely more painful than the cough which choked it. Then, "Fifteen hundred! Oh, my—! And Beezy here this morning with two thousand—"

"*Beezy!*" there was shriller panic in the shadow-man's cry. I thought he took out a handkerchief; mopped his forehead. "*He was here—*"

Again the thin needles of laughter, too painful for merriment.

"But you can't do this to me, Sal," the man on the veranda was gesturing frantically. "I got a family, Sal—grown boys—grandsons! Think of my wife—she never done you no harm. Three thousand—!" the voice broke. "I brung it with me. All I could raise, Sal—ain't that enough—?"

The answer came cutting through the door, the thin tone of a woman's daggering mockery that twisted in the man's shadow and made it writhe. "*You* never could raise enough. Not *you!* Never, never, *never!* Go *away!*"

The silence lasted an hour, or so it seemed to me, before I saw the man turn away from the door and move, bent-shouldered, leaden-footed, across the darkened clearing, fading among shadows on his slow way to the road. Then I saw something else—something that froze me to an image where I crouched. Eyes! Eyes like wizard's goggles in a clump of brambles on the opposite side of the clearing. Someone else had been watching that scene!

A LAST beam of daylight infiltrated down through the pines on that side, and what I saw was the refraction from a pair of glasses, round spectacles trained at the shanty with the fixity of aimed binoculars. The figure retreating to the road in stooped hopelessness did not know of that levelled espionage. Footsteps faded in the woods; the ambushed eyes watched.

I waited. Barely enough light remained to see those glasses emerge from their hiding place, move as disembodied shines toward the veranda, melt with the night at the shanty's front. Again I heard that clandestine knock, a low-voiced summons, faint answer from within. When the parley reached "four thousand dollars," matching almost word for word the dialogue I'd heard before, it became too astounding for belief. Only this bespectacled visitor was named Snowshoe, and he begged for the happiness of his youngest daughter who was going to be married.

His petition fared no better than Ginger's. His voice, deeper than Ginger's, conveyed a similar impression I'd heard it somewhere before, became a threatening rumble. "But you won't get away with this, Sal? Hear? I know what you're up to an' I warn you you better think twice—!"

"You're funny, Snowshoe," the voice from the house was crystal scorn through the night. "You and Ginger! And Beezy! Oh—what fools—!"

"Sal, if you keep on with this thing!"

The voice behind the door was acid then—vitrol. "Do you think you can harm a body who's *dying*—? Oh, my—! And you and all your picayune money. Is that all you think you're worth? The lot of you? Get out!" The thin up-pitched voice was almost strangling. "Go! The doctor'll be along any minute—if you don't want him to see you—*run!*"

I could hear the man running. Blundering off in blind darkness among the clearing stumps. But he stopped half way to the road to look back; his voice was raging, throttling in furious sobs; I couldn't see him but I knew he was shaking his fist. "You can't keep this thing up, Sal! We'll stop you, so help me, Hanna! Four Corners won't stand for no *witch!*"

There wasn't a sound in the night for a long time after those feet were gone. Shanty and woods were absorbed in total black. I crouched there with my neck-flesh crawling, skin twitching off a feel of decay. There was a creeping death in that invisible house, and something more ghastly. I wanted to get away from there, and it took an owl-hoot to start me home.

When I looked back once through the pines, I saw a light in one of the windows; a shadow through the shutter-cracks of a woman sitting there, the silhouette of a hand moving a pen. The respectable lights of Four Corners looked pretty good to me when I crossed the valley bridge, and I wondered if that whole ugly seance had been in my mind. Even so, I couldn't have imagined the grim shape of things to come, the curse that was to haunt Blue Valley for a month, the dreadful throw-back to witchcraft—

KNOWING what I knew, it was surprising that until the final storm I remained so short-sightedly in the dark and saw certain happenings which followed my evening excursion only as blind straws in a wind.

Mordecai Sailor's prize bull died the day Mordecai went to Brockton with a load of alfalfa; the veterinary said it had been poisoned, he wasn't sure by what. It was Mordecai's wife who found, wound like a thread around the bull's nose-ring, a strand of red hair.

Peter Johnathan's orchard had been blighted the week before; the day after the acute indigestion of Mordecai's bull, Peter found on his back stoop an apple pie, nobody knew how it got there, its crust unappetizingly threaded with red hairs. Nobody ate the pie; examination found a baked crow at the bottom.

Little Amy Watters had scarlet fever. Morning after quarantine strands of red hair were found glued to her bedroom window.

The letter sent to Postmaster Crackenbush from Valley Spring was filled with poisonous black spiders and red hair.

I began to hear these stories as one begins to hear rumors of smallpox in a neighborhood, rumors of a secret-spreading plague, little whispers of wind. I couldn't see the forest for the trees. This Hallowe'en stuff seemed nonsensical. Farmers today with their radios and ice machines aren't the simple rustics of David Harum's era; nobody could be scared by these dark-o'-the-moon capers into an Inquisition with bell, book and candle.

But what was the woman up to? Time and again, drawn by the sort of horror which repels as it fascinates, I found my eye scanning that distant ridge for the rooftop lonely in the pines. The creature dying in that desolation, consumed by that eating cough and subsisting only on a thin pain of laughter—what spell did she hold over those three shadowy visitors, the unknown Beezy, Ginger and Snowshoe? What power over their pocketbooks to bring them groveling—"Ginger" in the name of his family, "Snowshoe" for the sake of a marriageable daughter. Casual inquiry divulged no such names among my valley neighbors—any number of whom possessed grandsons, wives and eye-glasses. Who could they have been? Why the offerings at her door? Was this outcast in possession of something more evil than Siren sorcery; had she brewed with the dregs of her life some spiritual menace with which, from her house of exile, she could threaten the homes in the valley?

Someone, I knew, was fighting back. I discovered this one morning at the sheriff's office when, going there to renew my fishing license, I heard him arguing in the next room over a telephone. The telephone's voice was a buzzing of anger; and the sheriff was loudly agreeing, "it's a dang shame."

"Yessir," he said, "a downright disgrace. But there ain't a thing we can to about it long as she owns th' property outright, an' her taxes is ten years paid up. If her livestock was infringin', for instance—but she ain't got any, ner as far as anybody knows she ain't been trespassin'. No, you can't oust a body not for keepin' up their property—eh?—nobody's *seen* her leave th' premises. You gotta have *proof—!*"

And two nights later, a group formed around the doctor who was having his oil changed in front of Lem's: "Say, Doc, how's Frivolous Sal?"—"I don't discuss my patients."—"Well, now

look, Doctor. Some of us don't think it's right, her left up there
alone, dying like that, starving maybe. I took her up some veg-
etables yesterday and she absolutely refused to answer the door;
she's got it barricaded inside with a plank, her windows nailed
down and herself shut in like in a fort. I say, if the woman's gone
crazy—"

The doctor answered tartly: "I didn't know you were a charity
worker, Barrows. Didn't know anyone around here would go
near her place. I been seeing she gets enough to eat. And I
assure you her mind is very clear."

Wind whispered out of the doorway at the post office—three
ladies, hats roosting together: "Tell you, Melissa, any woman
who's shut herself up for five years ain't right."—"My husband
was sayin'. Plumb out of her mind, playin' such tricks."—"Floss
Watters is scairt to death, what happened to her Amy."—
"Lawyer Bickle says if Mordecai Sailor was public-minded he'd
demand she be put away, 'stead of keepin' his mouth shut."—
"Tell you, Melissa, these goin's on may be work of th' hand, an'
I say, maybe not. You never can tell, I say. You never can *tell!*"—
"If she *is* crazy it wouldn't be so bad as if she *ain't*—!"

Little conferences at the Feed Store grew to lowpitched
arguments at Charlie's Cafe. Men stood with heads close, dis-
persing quickly at the approach of some woman or a stranger.
I could sense the falling barometer in the way I was left on the
"outside" of this topic, relegated to my status of newcomer.
"Mule," I asked the gaunt farmer whom I knew as a confidant
of mine, "what's up?"

He shook his head. "Honest, I don't know. I asked some of
my crowd at Legion meeting the other night, but none of 'em
seem to know. Talk, I reckon. Just because that woman has red
hair—"

He spat sensibly. Mule keeps a stubborn head.

I thought I knew what was up; it was the "why?" that both-
ered me. I'm sure there were many in Four Corners as startled
as I at the way the storm broke in town meeting that eventful

Saturday night. Saturday night in Four Corners is Saturday
night in any country town: Farmers in from everywhere. Dusty
cars lined up at the curbs. Grange Hall open wide, and the town
clerk calling the council to order in the room downstairs, his
tone promising the audience nothing more important than a
debate on taxes. Mule Lickette (I wasn't there) told me the hall
was packed like a cabbage bin; farmers from as far as Valley
Spring—nobody seemed to know how or what, but every man
there had a feeling something was going to happen.

AND SOMETHING did. In the cottage across the street. *Little
Amy Watters died!* The gavel hadn't struck when the stricken
child's mother came screaming into Grange Hall, wailing her
anguish through the crowd. *"She did it! Her!* Her with her
wicked devil-taken soul. Her with red hair!"

Chairs going back. Shouting. Watters fighting through the
pack to carry out his fainting wife. Mule said that for a minute
you couldn't hear your own voice. Then, white and panting in
the door, fisting his way down to the rostrum, there was the
doctor come from the cottage across the street. Doc Trosch
flinging up his hands. Shouting for silence. Then:

"Listen to me, all! The child died of scarlet fever! You hear
me? Scarlet fever and nothing more!" He whirled on the platform; pointed at one of the older councilmen. "I've heard some
crack-potted stories these last few day: You, Banker Barrows.
I call on you as one of our prominent citizens—our *most* prominent citizen. Do you believe in witchcraft?"

Mule told me Barrows' face was bone-white as he stood up.
"Certainly not! There ain't no such thing! But I believe if th'
woman's crazy, if she's runnin' loose at night playin' these heathen
tricks—"

Dr. Trosch faced the crowd. "I can tell you that woman isn't
in condition to *leave* her house. I tell you, she's dying. Something
more! Some of you been imputing her sanity. Lawyer Bickle
come to me sayin' some clients of his demand she be put away.
As commissioner of Public Health of this district I'm tellin'

you, she's sane, an' I'll declare her as such." He paused with lifted fist. "One thing more. I got no call to defend that woman or what she was or is. No business of mine, either way. But she's my patient an' she's dyin'. Any move made to molest her it's my professional duty to call th' police. You there, Sheriff Vickers! You don't take the proper steps in this case. I'll be bound to advise the State Troopers."

You could hear the pocket watches ticking in Grange Hall as the sheriff stood up to speak. His face was like chiseled granite, his eyes pale bleak; instead of wearing the big nickle-plated star on his vest where he usually wore it, it was pinned that night on his coat lapel.

"Doc Trosch is right!" he boomed at the room. "I don't like this woman in our community, neither. I'm not forgettin' her criminal record. But long as there's no legal way to oust her, I'm bound as officer of th' law to see she stays. I've heard as how certain people been hinting they're goin' to take this matter in their own hands. Got a letter this afternoon warnin' me if anything happens to keep my eyes closed. You people know me better'n that. I was born an' raised in this valley, an' I've allus stood for law. Don't start nothing that's outside the law, or I'll be against you. That's all!"

You could hear the pocket watches ticking again when the sheriff sat down. Then somewhere in the night outside an open window, harsh, a bolt from the black, came an answering shout. "You may think that's all, Sheriff, but it ain't. Callin' th' law after the crime's been done, is lockin' th' barn after th' horse is stole! Our homes is more important than your law! Waitin' till after th' lies are told will be too late. Maybe you didn't read today's paper from Albany an' see there's a newspaper man coming to Four Corners tonight." The harsh voice trailed off. "What do you think he's comin' for—?"

Never, Mule Lickette assured me, had there been such a meeting in Grange Hall. The stampede to the window broke it up. Nobody knew who'd shouted out there in the dark, or why. Nobody knew what anything was about after that. Sheriff

Vickers had raced off in his car. Men were still standing the curb in baffled groups, waiting for something to happen. Doc Trosch had gone. Theodore Seymore was in possession of the little Watters girl. Mule Lickette had run, panting, over to my cottage to tell me about it.

"Witchcraft. Insanity. Threats. Newspaper man. All tied up with Frivolous Sal." He shook his head, going out. "It sure beats me."

It never occurred to me to link the "newspaper man from Albany" with my friend Lion, whom I'd invited up for a Sunday's fishing. That he might have inserted a note in his column (lucky he didn't mention my name) about his intended jaunt, never came to my thoughts. Nor could I figure a newspaper man into the thing until Lion, himself, came racing into town about midnight; landing in my door-yard with a load of Scotch and fishing tackle and wanting to know how long Four Corners had had a Black Legion.

"What do you mean, Black Legion—?"

"Took a wrong fork across the valley," he grinned at me, "and ran plunk into 'em on a side road. Saw 'em right in front of my headlights. White sheets and black hoods, and almost scared me into the middle of next week. They ducked off into a berry patch though, and I got on the main road darn quick afterwards. Probably just some prank going on, but—"

"Lion," I said whitely, "that isn't any prank. Come on!"

CHAPTER IV

I SHALL NOT soon forget that night-scene in the pines. Lion had driven a steeple-chase across the valley; we left the car on the lower road and took the shortcut up Blueberry Hill on foot, scouting up behind the prowlers (fortunately) but still in time.

The clearing was done in shades of black, blue and blue-black; the pines were carbon monoliths upholding a sky of crepe; the shanty a silhouette inked into a background of midnight. Only its roof was tombstone gray, touched faintly by the luminance of a moon that hung like a green dial in the pine tops, suffusing the outer edges of the scene with a cloudy aura of disaster. The silence was that of a vault. But my skin told me that, on the fringe of the clearing, Lion and I were not alone. Others there had heard us; played possum to listen? I suppose they thought we were some of their party, for the stillness was finally relaxed by a low whippoorwill call, a leafy rustling in the dark across the clearing.

A whippoorwill answered on our side, and at once the clearing was alive with sheeted figures, a phantom congeries thefting about in the dark. There may have been less than twenty, but the shadows multiplied them to an Indian band. Dim hand-lanterns, ominously shaded. Heads faceless under black gunny-sack masks. Fists weighted with clubs; one beckoning to the others with upraised buggy whip. Moving in from all directions, they converged in a creeping circle on the shack's silhouette, and the sweat broke cold on my forehead when I saw two with axes and a hand bearing a coil of rope.

"Lion!" I gasped. "They're going to luh—"

His fingers in the darkness gripped my arm. "Don't move."

"But we can't just *watch* here—"

His voice tiptoed up to my ear. "Can't make a move yet. There's a man on guard by that tree over there. With a gun—"

He wasn't a fly-cast distant. Standing so immobile, so utterly black and still, he seemed one with the pine. Peering, I could discover the shine of a shotgun barrel like a thin thread of moongleam taut between unseen fists. Lion was right. There might be a dozen of these vedettes deployed around us in the night. We hadn't a show with these ghosts; could only watch their ghost-show which had moved to the shanty's veranda. A fist knocking on that door. Softly. Louder with impatience.

"Sal—! Wake up, Sal! It's Beezy!"

No answer. I could see a redistribution of the hand-lanterns on the veranda, the shack-front only darker for their being there. The knocking quickened to pounding. "Wake up in there! This is Snowshoe, Sal! You hear? I and Beezy want to talk to you!"

Silence. No reply from the one emprisoned in that framework of a misspent life locked in a hermitage of decaying wood. On the door there were angered hammer blows; the summons breaking into a chorus of shouts.

"We know y're awake in there, Sal!"—"Come out peaceable, or it'll be the worse for you!"—"You know what we're here after, Sal, an' you hand it over to us, we won't molest nobody!"—"Fetch it out, Sal!"—"You open that door an' let us have it, or we'll come in there an' get it an' you, too!"

And you, too! I've heard a man's voice on that deadly basso before, but the baying of a dozen such voices cooled my blood. I was sure the woman, hearing that baying threat, would disperse them simply by giving them whatever they were after. But she gave no sign of having heard, answered with no window light, no voice. Shack and its darkness remained adamant. The shanty's inner hush merely deepened with the clamor raging at its door.

"Break her in then, boys! Wants to wreck our homes, does she? We'll learn the red-headed she-devil a lesson!"

LION had disappeared. Unable to bear the first axe-crash, I had spun to shout at him; capped my mouth with a hand when I saw he wasn't there. Vanished! The axe crashed again before I saw where he was—crawling on hands and knees, soundlessly, toward that invisible gunman by the pine. Lion has nerve. But his assault was stayed by an unexpected bellow from the gunman.

"Stop! Hold on, there!"

The figure made no swerve in Lion's direction, but plunged from wood's edge into the clearing; raced at the hooded mob with menacing gun. I glimpsed the nickel-plated star before the vandals gave back a yell.

"Sheriff Vickers!"

"Git away from that door, all o' you! This here's against th' Law! Ain't gonna be no lynchin' in Four Corners long as *I'm* Sheriff!"

"Now, look here, Vickers—!"

"Git offa that veranda, I tell you! I know th' lot o' you—want to, I'll call you out by name! Get outa here!" He was doing what no stranger could have done, shouldering through them with burly violence, threatening them with exposure more than gunfire. Chopping broke off. Dimmed lanterns retreated in an angry circle. Right then I took off my hat to that sheriff; there was no mistaking the temper of that crowd. He had my silent applause when I saw him square off before that door, legs apart, gun hugged to chest, indomitable statue of Law holding mob fury at bay.

"Vickers," a harsh voice challenged, "you know what sort this woman was!"

"Yes, I do," loudly. "But that ain't anything to do with th' law in question. I know she's an ex-jailbird an' public disgrace. Bad reputation all her life. You git a legal writ, I'll hustle her outa this county quicker'n you. But until I got legal warrant—"

"Lissen, Vickers," the harsh cry flung back, "we ain't gonna allow that red-headed vixen in there t' ruin our lives just becuz you can't find no law to stop her! We men are all good citizens, Vickers! Elected you to pertect our homes! You can't do it, we'll do it ourselves!"

"We got wives an' families," another shouted. "Duty t' them!"

"I told you at town meetin'! You get proof, get a warrant—"

"An' I told you," the harsh spokesman interjected, "that'd be lockin' th' barn after th' horse was stole. That woman knows there ain't no red tape to stop her. Knows th' only way to prove, is to let her go ahead. An' that'll be too late. Lot of us in this valley cherish our good names! Maybe this don't concern you, Vickers, but some of us don't want our lives an' homes muddied up with a lot of scandlous stories. People believe such stuff even when you can prove it's all lies. After th' lies are told, y're licked!"

"Yah," echoed another. "An' th' woman's dyin'. She figgers she'll pass out afterwards so's nobody could contest her for libel in court—"

"Whole valley's with us, Sheriff! You keep out!"

"We want that writin' of hers, Vickers! That's *her* witchcraft! Are we going to let her sell out our names with a pack of lies to the papers—?"

I got it! I got it from that last harsh shout, the key to all the other puzzle fragments—the things I'd heard and witnessed, the rumors, the part of the "newspaper man"—fitting at one sweep into the whole dark picture. "Lion," I gasped at him, "they think you've come here to buy—"

A blow on the veranda froze my tongue. Someone must have thrown a club. I heard the sheriff bawl, "Nobody's gonna get through this door!" Somebody squalled, "At him!" There was an instantaneous scrimmage on the veranda, grunts, oaths, trampling of boots, thudding of clubs, fists. Shadows scuffled around the black doorway, swarmed across a railing that fell in splinters, piled up on the ground. A voice shrilled, "He dassent shoot us!" Another, "I got the shotgun!" Another, "Bust into th' house!"

I'VE SEEN no man fight as the sheriff fought then. For a moment or so, robbed of his Winchester, he knocked those masked vandals around like a cyclone in a field of wheat-shocks. In the dim kaleidoscope of weaving lanterns, I could see the swinging bludgeons, the tumbling bodies, the sheriff centered in a thresh of dark figures, slugging, beating them back, throwing them off. The two with axes started for the door, and he caught them by the collar, kicked them headlong away. "Nobody gets in there! Nobody!"

Like wolves they were at him. Tackling his legs. Clubbing his back. His fists were mauls cracking on their masked heads. Three times the assault reached the veranda; three times in bull-like fury he drove them off. "No, damn you! I'll break yer necks, first! You ain't—gonna—get in!" Ten to one they were on him, a pile-up of sheets, flailing arms, kicking hobnails.

Lanterns smashed. Clubs splintered. His fury grew with theirs; he put up a one-man exhibition of slugging and jiujitsu that held me in the paralysis of an onlooker. Back and forth in shadows the battle raged. He was down. He was up. Down. Up again. A roaring red ruin of a man, face hammered crimson like something on a forge, eyes striking sparks, he drove those attackers a fourth time from that silent door. Drove them away from the veranda in a swirl of battle that circled among the clearing stumps.

It was there he went down. Free of the tangle, the two with axes had run to a front window and were smashing in frenzy at the heavy shutters. Thinking of the woman who must be crouching in that black and storm-shaken house, I forgot I was watching until I saw Lion in the middle of that fight. Somehow I was with him, then, plowing and punching in the dark flurry, and so we were there to see the sheriff go over like a felled ox from a crowbar on the skull—and both front and center for the battle's end. This came with the breaking of the window; the shearing away of those sinister blinds; and the scene was revealed as a picture in the open frame.

I won't soon forget the cry of the axe-man whose vandalism uncovered that picture. How those masked attackers, charging forward to see it, took root and stood staring in sudden hush. That hush might have been the stoppage of all sound everywhere that night. If Lion and myself had been noticed, we were then forgotten. In the minds of those around us there must have been older remembrances. I wonder what the masked memories of those masked citizens saw in that window-framed picture. I wonder—

All I know is what I saw. I don't know what I'd expected of that hermit's shanty or its occupant—what manner of redhaired Roaring-Nell termagant her history had painted in my mind, or what sort of witch's den I'd expected her retreat to be. I know I hadn't expected, in that raffish outer hulk of a house, a setting clean as a pin—the chair with crocheted chair-arms. the china visible on a back wall, the little vase of wild flowers, an interior dainty as a music-box making background for a portrait by Whistler.

He couldn't have done it. The moon drifted out of the pine tops and touched the portrait with a silvery luminescence, softening out the shadows with a deft and kindly brush. In profile she was posed, as natural in her chair as real life; had been content there for some time, one would have said—the clock on the old-fashioned writing desk having stopped three hours before. The shawl drawn over her shoulders was a delicate tracery of fine lace, and the same infinite patience must have made the patchwork quilt about her knees, the white embroidery on her cuffs. There was the sewing basket on the footstool beside her chair, a wicker bowl filled with spools and colored yarns, pin cushion, thimbles, crochetting needles. But she had put this aside for the ink stand and Spencerian pen, and then, having finished with her writing, fallen asleep at the desk so naturally one saw that a touch would have waked her and set her fumbling for her glasses.

I hope to always remember the fragility drawn in that figure, the composure in that sleep-smoothed profile—head bowed a little, features relaxed, the gentle smile of one released from another day's care. The silver-white of the moon-brushed hair; the delicate lines of age. Her hands, on the desk before her, were folded on the yellowed cover of what looked like a time-worn scrapbook; she had just made her last entry.

It was at least three minutes before I realized why no tumult and no shouting. no furious chopping of axes could have waked her. One by one the men around me were taking off their hats. Then, somehow, it was the spectacles in her lap that touched me most.

But it wasn't until that harsh voice—harsh as a bad cold, now—spoke out to the other "citizens," not until then had I realized Frivolous Sal was dead.

"The first man here who makes a move to touch that *diary*—!"

They had come to rob their own memories—not a white-haired old lady in death. The most ungallant there would not have disturbed those folded hands. Too bad Sheriff Vickers was not awake to see that picture—to see his fellow citizens lowering their heads before it, backing in respectful hush; moved, by the same pack instinct which had brought them ravening, to an act of restitution, sincere if late: "Alone up here for five years!"—"Hardly seen her since she come back from—from prison!"—"We'll send Seymore up, first thing in the morning."—"Have him arrange a right good service."—"I'll give a hundred dollars for th' parlor an' flowers."—"Don't care what my wife thinks, here's fifty."—"Count me in on that, Joe."

But I don't think the sheriff came-to until he heard them nailing up the broken window. He must have watched, and wondered why they were leaving. He made no interference, and nobody remembered him. He was not there when the masked party crept away. They went in silence, shamed, and they left the old lady at her desk where they'd found her, asleep, alone, but no longer in exile.

I HAD not been asleep five minutes when I woke with the fire-call wailing in my ears, and for a moment I thought it part of a dream. Then I grabbed my corduroys and fled.

It had been my honor to be elected to the volunteer fire department, and who would turn down a chance to run with the Protectives? The pay was glory; but if you missed the truck at headquarters you were fined a dollar. I would have let them fine me five-hundred dollars for missing the run that night.

Without looking, I knew where that fire was. Red smoke up on the ridge across the valley confirmed my fears.

Scarlet and clanging, we rolled for Blueberry Hill ahead of half the village, our careening pumper a comet followed by a speeding tail of flivvers, farm trucks, bicycles and barking dogs. Charlie Rambow (never guessing himself the incendiary) drove; and Charlie, once in a fireman's helmet, lost all respect for time and space. We got there. But he might as well have saved us the risk of broken necks.

The ridge-top was Fourth of July. In the night above the clearing, sparks swirled and climbed like the fairy lights of a roller coaster, and the tumult in the pines was lower carnival.

Driven off by the golden heat, we stood as helpless onlookers, our red hats held at bay, extinguishers useless; a lockjawed, sober-faced little company on the edge of Inferno. We knew what was in that crumbling mound of molten embers. But I think I, alone, of my fire-hatted companions knew she was dead; saw her shanty as a funeral pyre. And then I was wrong. It remained for our astounded eyes to learn whose crematorium it was—certainly it wasn't what I had expected!

Doc Trosch had saved her. Driving his late-night rounds, he had arrived just in time; smashed through the burning front window to snatch her out of the flame's reach—saving, too, the little time-yellowed book he had spied beneath her folded hands.

We came on them out on the wagon road—the doctor, the quiet old lady, and a State Trooper who'd beat the volunteers on the run. Doc Trosch was declaring his patient the victim of murder, and I think the acrid old physician was disappointed when he had to say, after examination, that she had died some time the previous afternoon, neither from violence nor smoke-stifled lungs.

Nothing we could do after that but wait for the embers to cool, and smother them at last under chemical. All of Four Corners was there by the time we set to work with our hosing. So all of Four Corners was witness to our finding of the body in the cistern.

The body of a man!

Running along the side of the house, he had fallen (as I once nearly did) through the rotted planking of the cistern-cover; broken his neck. Face up, he lay beneath an evil mirror of water that angled his neck askew, twisted his mouth, distorted his out-puffed eyes. Clutched in his left fist was the extinguished torch of arson; in the clutch of his right hand was a kerosene can. It was shocking to see the star shimmering under water like that—almost as shocking as the death-leer stamped on the dead sheriff's face. Nobody could understand why he'd burned her house down.

We had to wait for the answer until after we returned to the fire barn. The Trooper was there with Trosch. Charlie Rambow, Mule Lickette, my friend Lion, and myself were allowed to remain, hunting clues. The Trooper was turning the yellowed pages of the diary.

Therein we saw why Sheriff Vickers had so boldly defended her door—that he might, himself, destroy her girlhood biography before the others could see it:

> *January 3, 1897—He is coming to the house again. I can't bear the sight of him. Rather than marry him as father wishes, I would die.*
>
> *March 16, 1897—Father has told the village I am secretly engaged. That is to force me to go through with it. He says if I do not, the circumstances being what they are, it will cause a terrible scandal.*
>
> *April 21, 1897—Whatever can I do? Father has told me why I must marry T. Father owes T's father a great deal of money from gambling debts of long ago. If I refuse to marry T the debt will be brought in the open; father will be publicly disgraced. T holds it over me. O, God, help me!*
>
> *June 4, 1897—I can't. I can't marry a man I don't love, to pay my father's obligations. Have I no right to happiness? Father says the wedding must be next week. But I will run away. I will run away before they force me to marry Tom Vickers!*

There was that in the faded early pages of the diary. And there was also—

Not a line about Ginger or Beezy or Snowshoe! Not a mention of any of the valley's citizens! Not a breath or hint of scandal such as their imaginations had put in her pen, their warped little minds had fancied behind her refusal to sell them the recorded personal sufferings of a down-hill life—her desperate search for romance, her fiancé's death, her wartime marriage to a bigamist, her reckless abandonment of hope culminating in the Golgotha of a prison cell, as: *Dec. 24, 1925—I am learning to sew.*

But I am consoled by knowing that the rats who harried her, who tried to rouse mob feeling against her as crazy and a witch—I wonder to whom, in the romantic promise of youth, she had once given a lock of her flame-hued hair—I am consoled by knowing them as the sort whose inner consciences give them no peace.

Beezy. Ginger. Snowshoe. Quite by accident I came on those precious three in an old dim photograph among the cobwebs and forgotten horse-collars of the firehouse attic—volunteers themselves in 1897. Quite the boys with their Zouave shirts and curly sideburns; gay enough, in those days, for nicknames. The nicknames were scribbled under the photograph. On "Beezy" I recognized the beak-nose of Roger S. Bickle, Counsellor at Law. On "Snowshoe" the near-sighted glasses of Mordecai Sailor, master of Blue Valley Farms. In "Ginger" (pompous even then) none other than Leonidas Barrows, our County Bank.

So that was that.

At the funeral service for Clariselle Alders the minister preached on "throwing the first stone" and "judge not that ye be not judged."

It might not have been appropriate to the ceremony, but he could have quoted the last two lines of the old ballad that had given her her better remembered name. "A wild sort of devil, but dead on the level—" That was how Lion ended his prize-winning, hypocrite-searing article against lynching. It was an article that must have been read in excruciating discomfort by some of the citizens around Four Corners, who know the line "dead on the level"—even when Theodore Seymore has them in his parlor—will never apply to *them.*

|||

BARBER, BARBER, SHAVE A PIG

Blood is even thicker than lather.

"**NEXT—?**" **WILLIE UPDYKE** shook brown needles of hair off the white apron, and confronted the line-up sitting along the sidewall with somewhat the anxiety of a bull-fighter not too sure of his talent. Willie's eyes were timid blue; his chin the kind that retreated a little, as if it didn't wish to intrude. The rest of him was sort of like that, too. He waved the cloth limply; nobody seemed to notice him. The shop was fogged with the haze of cigars, cigarettes and corncobs; in addition, Anton Grunner was talking. When Grunner talked, everybody listened. Grunner's chin didn't retreat. It jutted from the lower part of his face like the prow of a German battleship, and said, "Listen, you!" It was a chin to end chins.

Willie Updyke repeated hesitantly, "Next—?" and Grunner's voice boomed, *"Ha, ha, ha!"* as if his battleship chin were firing. He was shaving himself as he laughed; dexterously whisking the razor around his guffawing jaw. He always shaved right after supper, no matter how many customers were waiting in the shop. Grunner shaved himself three times a day, and he took a lot of pride in the fact.

"Nobody neffer should see bristles on a *barber's* chin," he would boom at Willie Updyke. Especially evenings when he was on his way to call on Martha Teacher. That five-pound jaw would be dampish and rosy, steaming like something just out of a hot bath, massaged and perfumed and powdered.

"Ho, ho, ho!" He was pushing his great stomach against the

bottle-laden shelf to get his face closer to itself in the mirror; twinkling at himself and his reflected audience at the same time. "Yes, sir—!" he roared, lathering his chin with white fluff; then nimbly flashing the big ivory-handled razor. "Vould you belief it? I come into the shop and there's *him!* Standing there! All shrunk up and sweating! *Ha, ha, ha!* Just like a scared little rabbit!"

He was telling a story on Willie Updyke—a story he'd told at least a hundred times in the last two weeks. The whole village knew it.

"But that ain't all. *Ho, ho, ho,* no! You should see Villie after-vards! After they take poor Mister Henry Applegate's body away. It vasn't like the old man's face had been slashed. Two stabs in the heart didn't show. But ven Mister Sycamore telephones for a barber to come at vonce—"

A sickening dew came to Willie Updyke's forehead. Involuntarily his eyes went to the sign on the barber shop's backwall, the awful sign that had come to seem like a goblin horror held up before his flimsy spirit, a reminder and a taunt.

HAIRCUT—40¢
SHAVE—20¢
SHAVING THE SICK—50¢
SHAVING THE DEAD—$1.00

" '—vy,' I says to Villie, 'The undertaker vants a barber at his parlor right avay. I can't go on account of my hand still bleeding. Take your shaving tools, Villie, here's your chance to make a dollar.' *Himmelherrgott!* I go up there half hour later, and there's Villie sitting by the table all the lights on, poor Mister Henry Applegate's chin all covered with soap—mind you, the coroner had gone and the old man didn't look bad—and Villie vas shaking, yes—shaking so he couldn't hold the razor in his hand. No, poor Mister Applegate vould haff by now a beard so long as Kris Kringle's—so long as the murderer's, I tell you, if he vaited for Villie to shave him. I open the door. *Plunk!* He falls

right over on the floor. His face vas the whiter of the two. Yes, sir, the whiter of the two!"

It was the whiter of the two right then, turning toward Grunner in misery-impelled protest. "But I'd just seen him killed. Stabbed to death. Right in front of my eyes. Right there across the street on the steps of County Bank—"

GRUNNER'S face was an inch from itself in the mirror. Admiring its lathered chin. Pleased by its bulk and strength—giant strength that became, when transferred to the fingertips and when those fingertips held a razor, the delicacy of a jeweler. *Whisk!* Shaving a streak through snowy suds. *Zip!* Flicking out an ingrown hair. He slicked the last cream bubble from under his jaw, pinched his Adam's apple, shaped his chin with the moist loving fingers of a sculptor putting the finishing touches on an Apollo.

"Vat good," he bit into Willie's plaintive defense, "is any barber who loses his nerve? Shaving is not only a fine art, a barber, like a surgeon, must alvays haff a steady hand. Nervous people and razors don't mix."

"But Henry Applegate was my best friend," Willie Updyke

told the room desperately. "I was standing right there by the window when I saw—"

"And you vas still standing there," Grunner reminded him affably, "ten minutes later ven I came along." He paused to swaddle his chin in hot cloths, puffing. Five seconds steaming; then six seconds treatment with the fingertips. Then a dousing with alcohol, salve, cold cream, a final coat of talcum. The chin, when done, looked as plushy, as smooth and plump as a dimpled baby. Three times a day, and always before visiting Martha Teacher. It made Willie Updyke a little sick.

It bore around on Willie now, like some great pink menace, a thing that filled him, had always filled him, with cold dismay. He had never been able to stand up to the thrust of that soft-looking, powerful jaw that made a monumental base to the face of a grown-up Mellon's Food baby—the bud-like little ears, the sparkly eyes, the wheat-fuzzed, close-clipped head. To Willie Updyke that round pink bulge of chin was the focal point of everything loathsome. Grunner loved it, tended it so. It was Grunner's personality, the meaty embodiment of his driving character jutting out of his face.

Willie Updyke couldn't explain why something about that chin overrode him, mastered all his inner resistance, pinched something to death inside of him, beat him down. Why it made him stand like a fool before his neighbors as he was standing now, on exhibition for their scorn. A barber whose hand shook. Little Willie Updyke. Little Willie Updyke who stood looking through a window while a bank robber stabbed his best friend to death—

"Anyhow, Villie can still cut hair." Grunner always became genial after a shave, like a tomcat purring after washing its face. His manner toward Willie became more indulgent, the tone an adult might take with a child who wasn't quite responsible. "How about it, Villie?" Palms on his hips, he wheeled, twinkling down. "Do I pay you to stand beside an empty barber chair? Maybe you paint stripes on yourself an' be the barber pole out in front. Customers are vaiting, Villie," he reminded him patiently. "Customers."

Willie Updyke swallowed, "I said 'Next' twice—"

"Sure," Grunner nodded. "They didn't hear you." He blinked at the chair line amiably. "Villie can serve you, gentlemen. Next?"

Nobody in the chair line moved. Like tintypes in a family album they sat, arms folded, legs crossed, expressions rigid in dispraise. Luke Adams was grinning derisively. Simon Tinney openly sneered. Horace Johns looked across the top of the *Police Gazette* at Willie as if he didn't see him. Perspiration broke and ran down Willie Updyke's face. Were these old neighbors of his, these old customers refusing to patronize his chair? From the corner of his eye he could see Grunner, dabbing his muscular arm into the sleeves of his white-starched coat, watching this charade in round-eyed surprise. Grunner might fire him for this; certainly he wouldn't keep a barber nobody would patronize. His stomach ached in panic. He couldn't let that happen; he *had* to stay here—

"Shave?" his quaver was close to pleading. "Haircut, anybody—?"

Simon Tinney stood up. "Shave!" he said curtly, Then, looping his neckwear on a hatrack, he walked straight for the other chair, Grunner's chair. Passing Willie Updyke, he said across his shoulder in a flat voice loud enough for all to hear, "I'm not chancin' my neck with a guy so nervous he can't run acrost a street to help his friend fight off a bandit."

Willie Updyke felt as if his throat were stuffed with cotton. He wanted to speak and couldn't. Tears welled in his eyes. Through the blur he could see the faces in that line-up of tintypes approving Simon's outspokenness. Only Mule Lickette wasn't condemning him; the sober gravity on the farmer's gaunt face seemed worse. Reproaching him for not asserting himself, standing up, being, for once in his life, a man.

"Trim," he muttered, walking forward to take the vacant

chair. "Just a little off the sides, and some of that quinine tonic. Hurry it up, Willie, I got a date."

Grunner's kindliness was worst of all. "Villie"—his tone now conveyed a strong man's sympathy for another's weakness—"I see no quinine tonic on the shelf here, Villie. Yesterday I told you to fetch out a fresh bottle—Mister Lickette is in a big hurry—go down to the cellar and get some quickly, Villie."

THE CELLAR door at the back of the room was a thousand Polar miles away. He had to walk the whole distance past a thousand icy eyes. He had to pass under the sign—*SHAVING THE DEAD—$1.00*. As he closed the cellar door behind him, he heard Grunner saying in deep tolerance, "Ve mustn't be too hard on Villie; after all, it's hard to know vat you'll do ven you're up against a killer vith a knife in his hand." Willie Updyke did not dare look back. There were times when Grunner's eyes were like quick blue sparks, and Willie Updyke was terrified lest they might burn their way through to his thoughts.

The hog! The great, smiling, plush-chinned hog! A time might come, Mister Grunner, when that chin of yours—A time might come when that dollar shave—

He had hated the man from the moment he set foot in Four Corners. It wasn't so much that Grunner had come here to buy him out after his own incompetence had forced him to sell the shop (and hired him back with the large philanthropy of someone allowing a bungling old servant to remain on the premises). It wasn't that Grunner was a better barber, a city barber who knew all the new tricks and blandishments, the shampoos, scalp rubs and dandruff-treatments that Willie had never learned. It wasn't even that Grunner, coming here from New York with his sausage accent and hearty confidence, had in eight years built up such a popularity as Willie, in a lifetime, had never commanded. Or even that Grunner had beamed his way into the affections of Martha Teacher to the extent of having first choice of books in her little lending library and candy store on Hill Street.

"I just don't like him," Willie had told Martha Teacher glumly, refusing to attend a party she was giving Grunner. "No, an' I never did."

"After all the things he's done for you—the nice way he's always treated you. Willie Updyke, I believe you're jealous!"

Jealous? The thought of Grunner's laughing big chin draped over Martha's lace collar (as he'd seen it through the porch vines one night) filled Willie Updyke with a sickness greener than any jealously. As for all the nice things Grunner had done— lending him money, asking him to go on fishing trips, buying him cigars and drinks—the man's constant generosities were bitter as wormwood and gall. Always they were forced on him so that he couldn't refuse. From the first, Grunner had seen to it that his beneficiary was the debtor and Grunner the munificent bestower of alms. But the man's attitude of big-hearted Dutch uncle, laughing at you one minute and sorry about hurting your feelings the next—that was most galling of all.

Like tonight. Guffawing out how he'd fainted in the undertaking parlor; showing him up before his neighbors as a weak-kneed namby-pamby too rabbit-souled to go to the aid of his best friend. Then, after his self-esteem was inwardly and publicly demolished, defending him against the community's scorn.

And what could he do about it? The man was built like Samson, as forceful as an express train. His personality crushed you, the way obstacles were crumpled by his laughter, dangers scattered by his jeers. There was a bull in Jed Rambow's pasture no farmer dared approach; just to show his contempt of such frailty, Grunner used to cross the pasture every Sunday on his way to the ball game. "The trouble vith you is, Villie," he would put an arm of friendly biceps around the shrinking shoulders, "the trouble vith you is, you're afraid. Me, anything I vant I get; nothing stands in my vay. You, all your life you dodge everything. You're afraid of Martha Teacher. You're afraid of bandits. You're afraid of yourself. *Donnerwetter!* you're afraid of me!"

He *was* afraid of Grunner. Terribly afraid. And he *had* been

afraid of that bandit; so afraid that he failed Henry Applegate
at the moment when he might, with courage, have helped the
stricken old man who was his friend.

IT WAS no use telling himself it had all happened too quickly
for him to do anything. No use telling himself he couldn't have
possibly got across the street in time. He could see it all now
on the underside of his pain-closed eyelids as clearly as a news
reel running across a screen. The portals of County Bank on
the opposite side of the street; the clock over the doors reading
ten. Monday night and the curbs deserted, white from a first
brief fall of snow. Grunner had gone to call on Martha Teacher,
and he'd been alone in the barber shop, standing unhappily by
the window like a boy kept after school.

He was honing Grunner's big ivory-handled razor, a shining
thick German blade that made him shiver at the touch because
of its association with Grunner's chin. It was the devil of a big
razor, heavy, sharp as a sin, and he was honing it very carefully
on the oily stone, apprehensive of a slip that would take his
fingers off like bits of cheese. He wasn't paying much attention
to the window.

And it had happened in a flash. Two flashes, really. The doors
of the bank bursting open. The old night watchman and his
assailant, locked together, stumbling down the steps. Only a
moment they grappled; in the dimness of the frosted street
lamp they were no more than flitting shadows. Two flashes as
the knife struck twice. Henry Applegate's body sinking down,
and the bandit crouching over it, fumbling over it like a gorilla
over its kill. The bandit turned around for one shadowy moment,
body crouched, knife dripping in his lifted fist; turned and
looked straight at Willie in the barber shop window.

That was when he should have charged out into battle, rushed
to the rescue of his friend. And he had stood—paralyzed by
that look—as if his knees were welded together, his boots frozen
to the floor. No good to remind himself the old man, stabbed
twice through the heart, was instantly dead. He hadn't known
it then, and he hadn't budged.

He would never forget that picture—Henry Applegate's shadow stretched on snow, the bandit a pantherish silhouette, the scene in black and white save where, under the watchman's flat profile, there was a single dreadful splash of red. He would always remember that momentary glimpse of the killer's face— not a face, either, but a sloppy black cap with brim low and ear-flaps down, mouth and chin hidden by a turned-up overcoat collar, and between collar and cap-brim, no features but a pair of smoked glasses. It had seemed as if those black glasses were all there was of the face, and his heart had turned to milk when he realized that dark-goggled gaze was directed at him. He couldn't take his own eyes off that red-tipped knife. Too late he remembered the razor in his own hand, and started for the door.

The killer had gone—melted back into the darkness of the bank. Only old Henry Applegate remained, lying there with stark unseeing eyes, two blowouts in his heart, and something clutched in his death-fisted hand. No use telling himself he hadn't chased the murderer because he thought to give Henry First Aid. He had knelt there by the body because he hadn't dared follow an assassin who left tracks in the snow that were merely elliptical blobs, more animal than human—who left such awful evidence in the victim's death-clutch. In that dead fist were strands of human hair. A barber ought to know about hair.

No one would ever know the resolution it took to pick one of those evil strands from the grip of a dead friend; examine it under a frosty light. No false hair, that, but a coarse human residue, oily and blue-black, about five inches long and yanked out by the roots—he could see the pinhead of the root where it had been torn out of the living follicle. It had turned him cold as a tombstone; made him forget the murderer was getting away. Held him in stiff paralysis until he was all at once aware of car-lights coming down the street, sound of a jogging motor, somebody coming.

He was back in the barber shop as if blown by a wind; stand-

ing at the window when the flivver stopped at the curb and
Grunner jumped out. Grunner didn't do any hesitating. Grunner
saw the body and yelled. Grunner did more than that. Shouting
for help, he dashed straight for the open doors of the bank;
charged through the black-hung entry like a lion going after a
tiger in its den. It wasn't quite clear what happened after that;
squalls came sailing out to the street, Grunner's shouts, sounds
of trampling, a savage howl. Then a trooper's motorcycle was
there; the street was an uproar of running men; half the village
arrived in its nightshirts; the bank lights blazed on.

THEY found the bank vault looted; the back door jimmied
open. They found Grunner cursing and groaning, nailed to the
wall by a ten-inch knife through the palm of his left hand.
Henry Applegate was dead with some black hairs clutched in
his fist; and the murderer was gone. "I almost had him," Grunner
was roaring. "I'd 've got him if he hadn't pinned my hand!"

Willie Updyke was glad he hadn't been there to hear the
cheers as they pulled out the knife and Grunner only grinned
at the pain. No, he could only stand like a clothing dummy in
the window while the crowd brought Grunner out a hero and
old Henry Applegate was taken away and his own footprints
were wiped out by the manhunt starting after the bandit's tracks.
He couldn't tell them how he'd run across the street too late.
He told them he'd seen the stabbing and he tried to describe
the bandit, but he couldn't explain about the strand of hair he'd
kept.

"No, sir, I don't recognize it," he told the trooper when shown
the tuft they'd found gripped in Henry's fist. "But I'll tell you
something. That bandit had a *cap* on! Wore low with the ear-
flaps down. Them hairs couldn't been yanked from his head in
that fight, so he must've had a beard!"

"Vy, sure he had a beard," Grunner was positive. "Didn't I
grab it ven I was fighting him there in the dark? A lousy thick
beard, too, and if I'd only had my razor I'd haff got some more
of it, I tell you."

And that was the trouble. That was what had struck him cold there on the steps on the bank. That was why he couldn't talk to anybody, why he couldn't tell the crowd he *had* run across the street, why he couldn't speak up to defend himself from the contemptuous eyes of his neighbors and Grunner's abhorrent pity. That was why, on the dark of the cellar steps, descending after a bottle of quinine tonic, his forehead was clammy at the memory and his knees were trembling.

On the bottom step he mopped his temples; groped for a light-cord; twitched on the electric bulb. Carefully he took from his pocket a small white envelope; plucked from the envelope a single black hair. A thousand times in the last two weeks he'd examined with aching eyeballs that greasy jet-black strand. A thousand times suspicion had grown to certainty—conviction of something he'd suspected from the first.

He'd seen that hair before. At some time in the past it had come into the barber shop!

It could only belong to one man, a low-browed animal of a man who drank clear alcohol and ate weasels, who roamed the woods alone for months of primitive hunting, who fought wolves with hickory clubs and had been known, single-handed and with nothing more than a hatchet, to kill a bear. It could only belong to that man, the one man in the valley Willie Updyke feared even more than he feared Anton Grunner. The black hair quivered in Willie Updyke's fingers; anguish distorted his forehead.

"But it can't be Medicine Joe," he moaned to himself. "There's others in the valley with black hair; I gotta keep tryin'. It *looks* like Medicine Joe's, but it just *can't* be!"

"Villie!" Grunner's hail came down the cellar steps. "Haff you gone into hiding down there? Mister Lickette is vaiting. Customers are coming in, Villie. Customers—!"

HE WAS glad there were new arrivals in the barber shop to create a diversion, and he tried to make his own presence more insignificant than ever, sidling down the room to his barber's chair and hastily setting to work on Mule's trim. Then he almost knocked over the bottle of quinine he'd juggled all the way upstairs. The very thought of Medicine Joe had his nerves as jumpy as popcorn.

Postmaster Crackenbush and Anvil Smith had just come in with excited faces and Albany newspapers, followed by Trooper Eddie McElroy. Attention was centered on the trooper, whose Harley-Davidson could be seen listing on its standard at the curb. Willie Updyke liked Trooper McElroy, but tonight the big fellow's grave countenance and worried tone awakened in him new alarms.

"Not a trace." the trooper was admitting reluctantly. "Nothing new yet, boys." He brushed flakes of snow from his coonskin cap, staring at the window angrily. "Looks to me as if the dirty rat's made a clean getaway."

"Nothing new about his tracks?" Luke Adams asked.

"Except he might've been wearing rags wrapped around his feet or something. The tracks wasn't shoes, boots nor arctics. Anyhow, he went out th' back door, same as he got in, an' waded into that creek flows behind th' bank. Whether he went up-stream or down, we don't know."

"Funny he got away like he did," Postmaster Crackenbush observed. "Wasn't five minutes from th' time he nailed Grunner's hand to th' wall that th' hull village was after him. Seems like he just vanished."

"That's it. He musta come outa th' stream somewhere. If he went south, though, he'd 've come to where th' creek runs in a ditch alongside th' highway; somebody'd seen him sure. Went north th' creek runs through pasture, an' we beat every inch of bank without a sign of tracks."

"How 'bout that tramp you picked up in Albany, Eddie?"

"Had a beard all right, but th' hair didn't match."

"That wrestler they had over to Brockton—?"

"Man Monument Sheehan? Time of th' murder, *that* guy couldn't break a scissors hold at a Brockton Legion smoker, much less come way over here and break into a bank. Every bum we pick up with whiskers has an alibi."

Horace Johns flung down his *Police Gazette*. "Then it's gone! All that money from the Dairymen's League. Forty thousand dollars. Half the savings of everybody in Four Corners!"

"Most of that was insured," Trooper McElroy snapped. "Poor old Applegate wasn't. It's th' murder we're sore about, Horace. Old Henry put up a good fight at th' last, when he found the alarm wires were cut. Tried to reach th' street to yell. Tried to save th' keys. It was a cold-blooded killing, all right. That bandit must've known the old man carried the keys to th' cashier's desk where they kept the combination to th' vault. You hear th' Bank Association's offered a ten thousand dollar reward, dead or alive? Th' dirty butcher—I hope it's dead!"

"Say!" Grunner looked up, squinting, razor in butterfly fingers at the top of Simon Tinney's chin. "Ten thousand dollars! Vell, I hopes it's alive. Giff me von chance at him for vat he did to my hand."

"Don't look like we'll see him alive or dead, either," Anvil Smith said acidly, "way the police are goin'."

"All we got to work on are a fish-knife you can buy in any hardware store, an' a half dozen hairs," the trooper protested. "Grunner couldn't see him in th' dark; and Willie, here, couldn't give much of a description, what he could see at night from fifty feet off."

Running the clippers around the back of Mule Lickette's thatch, Willie Updyke could feel his own neck reddening. "I couldn't see what he wore huh-hardly," he admitted meekly. "Just a dark overcoat an' black glasses an' a cap. But his cap was on all th' time, hidin' his face—"

"Like you was hidin' yours?" someone jeered; and all eyes in the room were censuring him again; even the oleograph of President McKinley above the row of armchairs looked disgusted. Trooper McElroy was turning in the doorway.

"Well," he said, "Grunner's the only man who got anywhere

near him so far. Sure is queer about that bandit's beard. We've canvassed every farm in th' valley an' can't find nobody who's seen a black-bearded man since Garfield's administration. Those hairs turned out to be genuine, an' they wasn't dyed. Killer probably wore th' beard for a disguise, and shaved it off right afterward; but th' point is, a guy with whiskers these days is noticeable, you'd think someone would've spotted such black ones *before*—"

"Ow—!" Interruption came from Mule Lickette, swooping up out of Willie's chair, fists to eyes. "Take it easy with that quinine tonic, Willie, you're pourin' it into my face. Stings like holy calliope!"

Towels. Water. Willie's right knee getting in his left knee's way, "I'm sorry, Mule. Honest I am—" Luke Adams sneering from a corner, "Whatsa matter, Willie? Nervous because Mule's got black hair?" Mule rubbing his eyes and laughing it off, and Grunner apologizing for him, and the tintypes along the wall contemptuous. But they didn't see him slip that hair back into his pocket.

Trooper McElroy had gone out, and Mule Lickette was going; facing that battery of hostile villagers, Willie felt as if his last friend had gone. If only he could shout out what he knew. If only he could tell them how these black-haired suspects were thinning like sand in an hourglass and narrowing down to Medicine Joe. If only the floor would open up and swallow him—Martha Teacher was coming into the shop!

"Bob," she declared herself briskly, smiling at the smoky room.

Somehow Willie managed to get it out. "Next—?"

For the second time that evening no customers made a move. Blindly he saw Martha nodding as if she understood; taking off her hat, coolly shaking out glints of auburn from her wavy warm hair. Grunner blinked up from an examination of Simon Tinney's dandruff, his smile as big as the moon.

"So sorry I am just now busy, Martha. In a hurry?"

She didn't even notice Willie Updyke. "No hurry at all, Anton. I can wait."

WILLIE UPDYKE'S stomach was a hard green apple under his belt, an indigestible lump of cold despair. He couldn't run, back out or hide. He could only stand there ignored beside his ignored barber's chair, neck cloth dangling, scissors out of work, despised, self-conscious and miserable, as horribly exposed as the boy he'd once been in a dunce cap on exhibition in the corner of a schoolroom; only this time it wasn't arithmetic but his whole life that lay around him in Zero—failure. Martha, Grunner, himself—it was as if the three of them were on a stage, with all the village for an audience, and as if suddenly, in front of everybody, he had vanished. They didn't see him. He wasn't there. Martha's glance touched him once with the disinterest she might have given a fence post, a milk can or a yella dog.

So she, too, had ticked him off as a failure. She was going to let Grunner trim her hair. Those moist pink fingers would be patting her auburn waves; that steamy plush chin leaning close. The thought sent a worm of nausea crawling through the green apple of Willie's stomach; he had to turn around, do something, busy himself with a razor strop lest Grunner would see his face. Grunner wasn't looking at him, though. Grunner was enjoying the limelight. In the mirror he could see Grunner beaming at Martha Teacher.

"Haff you heard the latest on the murder, Martha? Ten thousand dollars if you catch the killer. Maybe I try to catch the killer, myself."

Grunner would say it like that. Offhanded. As if he could just walk out and do it any time, but right now he had to give his attention to Simon Tinney's cowlick.

And of course Martha would gasp. The tintypes along the wall would sit up in interest. Anvil Smith exclaiming, "*Saay!*" Luke Adams staring big-eyed. Horace Johns blurting out, "You don't think you know who the man is—!"

"I don't know anything." Grunner's tone implied he knew a great deal. "But I been thinking. I been thinking the police vaste their time looking the wrong place. Albany. Brockton. Bah. I say it vas a local job."

"Y'don't mean someone right here in th' valley?"

"Vy not, Mister Tinney? Sure I do. Look. It had to be somebody who'd know about poor Henry Applegate carrying the keys, eh? Somebody who vatched the bank and knew ven big money would be on hand, too."

"Yeah," Luke Adams drawled puzzlement, "but how about that there beard? Ain't nobody in th' county with black whiskers, an' I reckon it's like th' trooper says, if anybody'd been growin' 'em, they'd been *seen*."

Grunner chuckled over a bottle of Bay Rum. "Vich don't mean a feller couldn't go avay and raise a beard. Look. Suppose he neffer vore von before, vat could be a better disguise. Off he goes for six months, ve'll say. Comes back with viskers. Robs the bank. Kills Applegate. Shaves aftervurds, and who knows him? Case he'd been seen, nobody recognizes him, and—"

Horace Johns was on his feet. "Bill Rambow! He's got black hair! Goes all summer traveling for his old man's lumber comp'ny—"

"Sure," from Anvil Smith, "only except the night old Henry was killed, my sister seen Bill at a movie show over in Boston."

Martha put in breathlessly, "But that doesn't mean Mister Grunner may not be right. Oh, Anton—if only *you'd* been in the barber shop that night instead of at my store! If *you'd* been here—"

Grunner told the room cheerfully, "I'd haff gone after him vith my razor, I told you. *Ha ha!*" He made brisk pantomime with his big ivory-handled blade, carving crisscross flashes through the smoke. "Instead of hairs for a clue ve might haff got the feller's head. Anyhow—you're next, Mister Adams— shave? Not too close? I giff it free if I nick von smallest drop of blood—Anyhow, I tell you von thing, my friends. Eight years

I been shaving everybody in this neighborhood, eh? Giffing shampoos and massages, too. Chins I know like my own. Faces. *Shapes* of faces!"

There was a dramatic pause. In the mirror Willie Updyke could see the shapes of the faces in the chair line, eyes on Grunner, expectant; Martha leaning forward, lips parted a little.

"*Shapes* of faces," Grunner grinned, letting it sink in. "And I had my hands on that bandit's face, see? For fifty seconds, maybe, but long enough. Even vith a beard, I tell the shape of the chin, the jaws, the cheekbones. Somewhere, I think, I haff felt that face before. Sometime in the past it vas in my barber shop. Sooner or later, it comes into the barber shop again, I can vait"—Grunner chuckled—"but I don't forget vith my hand. That feller thinks I vouldn't know him. Shave? *Ho ho!*" Slowly he drew the razor through a wisp of cigarette smoke. "A ten thousand dollar shave, eh, Martha? That vould be something!"

NOBODY noticed the man who stood in the doorway. Everybody was looking at Grunner, enthralled by the pantomime of that ten thousand dollar shave.

Like a shadow the man was there, coming in as quietly as the little gust of snowflakes that followed him through the door. Like the shadow of a low-browed animal of a man, a man who drank clear alcohol and ate weasels, who roamed the woods alone for months of hunting, fought wolves with clubs and had been known, with nothing more than a hatchet, to kill a bear. Feet apart, thumbs in belt, he made no interruption, but stood there, squat and bow-legged, dumbly watching the room, swaying a little. His eyes were cups of whisky in a face of jerked beef; the crimson flush to his complexion tinged the old knife-scar on his beardless chin with purple malevolence; a bottle jutting from each pocket of a ragged mackinaw told of the alcohol in that swaying stance.

Nobody noticed him. Nobody but Willie Updyke, who had felt the breath of that opening and closing door as a wind from Alaska blown through the marrow of his bones. He saw the

mirrored image of that smoldering, scar-jawed face as a visage
of Satan conjured in the glass. He saw the blood-circled eyes
aimed blearily at his barber's chair. He saw the man shake snow
from his wicked uncut mane of blue-black hair, and more
forward like a panther, implacable as Fate approaching in a
dream.

Back turned, Grunner was lathering Luke Adams' jowels,
talking loudly to an attentive audience. No one seemed aware
of crisis at the shop's front, least of all the big Dutchman who
was telling the world in general and Martha in particular just
what he could do to someone he didn't like with a razor. Between
Grunner and the newcomer, Willie Updyke felt as if he were
squeezed in a vise. The creature advancing on him made no
sound. His prowling tread was silenced by flappy hunting moc-
casins that left a splayed elliptical track which dried as soon as
it was printed on the linoleum.

"Haircut!" The low-growled word hit Willie's face like a gust
of gas. Flinging a crumpled mass of bills on the mirror-backed
shelf, Joe grunted, "Just sold heap of fox furs—more where that
came from!" He sat down in the barber chair.

"Gimme," he grunted at Willie Updyke, "everything."

Willie Updyke brought his hand from his pocket and dazedly
reached for the scissors, but even before he could match that
uncut mane with the single strand cupped in his palm, he knew
it was the same hair!

HOW he went through the motions of the next half hour, Willie
Updyke never knew. Clippers. Scissors. Shampoo. Wildroot.
Lilac water. Pomade. Somehow he was doing it, giving that foul
mop of hair everything—not just everything from Dr. Tarr's
Scalp Elixir to a dandruff singe, but everything he had left
inside of him, the last ounce of self-command he could summon
from a shattered nervous system.

The room was going round and round, and he had to think.
Grunner's voice was going on and on, and he had to forget that
huge jaw. Martha was in the room, not ten feet away, and he

had that to think of, too. And he had to hold this drunken devil in the chair somehow, hold everything in delicate balance because that wicked black head was as dangerous as a smoking bomb; and he must think of something, think fast before the explosion came off.

With Medicine Joe's squat body hidden by an apron, and the chair swung to face the front window, so that Willie stood between his customer and the sidelines, the job was only begun. "Little more off the top? Want it short, Joe?" Another handful sheared from that scalp and the man would resemble a convict, but the *snip-snip* of scissors was a screen for his low voice and his customer's grunted answers. "Sure. Got plenty money. You gimme everything."

"When—when's th' last time you were in for a haircut, Joe?"

"Spring. Other man, big man cut it. Twice a year. Okay?"

Then Willie asked huskily, snapping the scissors to keep the room from hearing, "Where you been all this fall, Joe?"

"Hunting. Woods." The answer came indistinctly through an offside roar of laughter from Grunner and Martha saying something and through the smoky air full of talk. Blood pounded in Willie's ears as he murmured, "Were you alone, Joe?"

"Don't I always hunt alone? Huh. Know where foxes go. Deep woods. Plenty foxes. I hunt alone."

"More quinine, Joe? Some of this here tonic?"

"Sure. Plenty perfume. I got money. Plenty everything."

Hair tonics. Lotions. Eau de cologne and mange cure. If the brute wasn't loggy from his liquor-bulged stomach, he must certainly pass out from all this sousing on his skull. But the fumes of that rich anointment made Willie's own head swim. He could feel his heart chugging like a threshing engine; as usual, in emergency, his mind had become a panic-stricken blank. He couldn't think of anything, and time was going, time was running away from him, he didn't know what to do and if he stalled too long he would lose his chance. Splashing hair tonic, he closed his eyes in a desperate effort at concentration, but all he could see was the portals of the bank across the street and a remembered dark figure crouched there with a bloody knife in its fist. It wore a cap and dark glasses; its overcoat collar was turned up to hide the lower half of its face. Henry Applegate lay dead with a tuft of hair in his fist, hair torn out by the roots. It couldn't have come from the killer's head because of the cap, so it must have come from his beard. Grunner said he'd had a beard. The murderer had raced back into the bank, and a few moments later Grunner had come up in his car, dashed into the bank, battled someone in the dark. Someone who'd knifed his hand to the wall. Someone bearded. Grunner said he could feel the shape of that face in the dark; said he could tell it again—

Willie Updyke's eyes stared open. The drumming in his ears had become so loud the vibrations were shaking him. He had to wait ten seconds for his hands to stop trembling. Then he wrapped a hot towel around his customer's head, draped a steamy cloth across his eyes, and said, tilting the chair to a reclining slant, "How about a massage, Joe? Like a massage?"

No answer.

"Joe—?"

A gentle, alcoholic snore.

WILLIE stepped to the shelf and picked up his razor. Deliberately he began to strop the blade. *Clippety-clap—clippety-clap.* Working with an industry that brought beads of perspiration out like blisters on his forehead. Mirrored in the long glass, the room assumed a weird perspective; Grunner's back, stooped over the next chair, seemed gigantic; the line of waiting customers far away. He could see mouths going, but the hammering on his eardrums muffled the talk to a meaningless drone. But he saw that Martha was watching him, now, frowning a little, her eyes going from him to the man wrapped up in the chair. He drew a long breath, and faced Grunner.

"Mister Grunner—"

"Vell, Villie?"

He must have interrupted a story, for the big pink face pouted irritably as it steered around, and he had to clear his throat to go on. "That bandit—in the bank you was fighting him in the dark—are you sure he had a beard, Mister Grunner?"

"Vat's this? Sure? Sure I'm sure. Didn't Applegate pull cut some hairs? Didn't I grab it, myself? Vould a barber know a beard or—"

"And tonight. When you said you could tell a face after you'd felt it once. People you'd barbered and such. You said you could tell that bandit's chin again, even if it did have a beard. You mean that, too?"

"Mean it? Vouldn't I remember faces I've worked on! Vouldn't my fingers feel? Every face and head has its own shape, not so?"

Willie wondered what the shape of his own face was like right then, the way everyone was glaring at it. Could they see his hair was on end? Words stuck in his throat, then stumbled out across his tongue in a voice he hardly recognized as his own.

"This man in my chair here, Mister Grunner—he'd like a massage—maybe you remember Medicine Joe. Comes to town about twice a year, spends th' rest of his time runnin' trap lines up Canada way. You're a better barber'n I am, Mister Grunner— reckon Joe'd like you to do it, if you understand me. Maybe you'd better massage his face, Mister Grunner—"

He saw a grin of understanding spread across the red plush countenance, the spark eyes glinting like points of flint. He saw the tintypes against the sidewall go rigid in astonishment; Luke Adams sitting bolt upright in Grunner's chair; Martha with one hand to her throat, startled and white. He saw Grunner slip the big ivory-handled razor into his pocket, reach for a jar of cold cream, walk slowly to the front chair and set to work with those dexterous fingertips, as if moulding the stupid clay of that sodden face. He saw the big man stare and bend lower and stiffen up.

"It's him!"

In the stunned silence of the next thirty seconds every breath in the room might have stopped—every breath except the whisky snuffle of Medicine Joe that exhaled an impervious snore. Grunner jerked the towel from the man's slumped head, and muttered, glaring down, "It's the bandit, all right—Look at that black hair! By golly, for vat he done to Applegate and me, I ought to cut his throat vere he snoozes, the dirty murderer!"

Willie Updyke gasped, "Are you sure?"

And Grunner snarled, "Didn't I haff him on the floor that night? Didn't I haff my hands on his face so I might recognize him in the dark, maybe? It's the same man, I tell you, I'd know him anyvere. Even if he's shaved like now every hair off his chin there vas something I could feel under his viskers that he couldn't shave off. That *scar!*"

Then the barber shop was swimming in circles again, and everything was out of perspective in Willie Updyke's focus. The effort to speak seemed to stop his heart. "Grunner," Willie Updyke whispered, "you're a liar!"

IT GREW. It swelled. It puffed and grew in Willie's vision until it seemed to loom over him as giant-sized as a storm cloud, all streaky maroon and purple, held in electric suspense above his head. In the blur of that apoplectic face the eyes were darts of lightning, the voice a mutter of thunder gathering to crash.

"I said I felt that scar under his viskers that night. Vat do you mean, I'm a liar?"

Willie felt like Jack at the foot of the beanstalk locking up at the ogre. Whispering. "Medicine Joe ain't the murderer. He was never in th' bank that night. Them hairs in Henry Applegate's fist belonged to Joe, all right, but they didn't come from his beard. Medicine Joe ain't got any beard."

"He's shaved it off, Villie," the thunder was coming nearer. "He had von the night he killed Applegate, and I grabbed him by it ven—"

"Medicine Joe was off in the woods that night, hunting alone.

Like he always goes around alone. Like you know he always goes alone—so he can't have no witness for an alibi." Willie cleared desperation from his aching throat. "Grunner," he panted, "where were *you* the time of the murder?"

It seemed a hundred years before Martha Teacher's voice came from somewhere. "Willie Updyke, have you gone crazy? Anton was in my store that night when—"

"It was ten o'clock," Willie panted. "The clock over the bank—it was ten o'clock when Henry was killed."

Martha's voice: "Anton was in my store at ten o'clock. I remember he showed me his watch and said he ought to be getting back and—"

"Maybe he'd set his watch a few minutes fast," Willie husked out. "Maybe it wasn't really ten o'clock till he busted in th' back of th' bank. He could've left his car up th' road a piece, hidden in th' dark where th' creek flows along th' highway. He could wade th' creek to around behind th' bank—"

"Willie Updyke, what are you saying?"

"I'm sayin' it couldn't've been Medicine Joe, but it *could've* been Grunner. I'm sayin' he could've stabbed Henry out in th' front, run back out th' rear, waded th' stream back to his parked car. I'm sayin' he could've shucked his disguise and driven up in front of th' bank and pretended—"

"Pretended?" Grunner screamed. "Didn't they find me nailed by a—"

"You could do it yourself," Willie Updyke whimpered. "You could've pinned your own hand to the wall. Make it seem like someone else done it, and a guy who'd murder a poor old man an' try to throw guilt on somebody else—yeah, to get a reward along with forty thousand dollars—"

"Herr Gott! Villie, haf you lost your head—?"

THE WORDS were sure to be his own death warrant, but he sobbed them out before fear could stopper his throat. "Who else could've pulled them hairs outa Medicine Joe's scalp some time when he was in here gettin' a haircut, drunk? Saved 'em in a bottle of hair oil or something to keep 'em fresh so's to plant on Henry to throw suspicion? But you forgot you was wearin' a cap, and so you had to agree they come from the bandit's beard—and since Medicine Joe hasn't any beard, why, you're lyin' about that scar and—"

He couldn't stand it. Always to Willie Updyke that round pink bulge of chin had been the focal point of everything loathsome. For eight years it had overridden him, mastered all his inner resistance, pinched something to death inside of him, beaten him down. Made him stand like a fool before his neighbors, as he was standing now. Little Willie Updyke who stood looking through a window while a bank robber killed his best friend. Little Willie, the barber, afraid of a chin—

If Grunner had kept on scowling—But the sparkly eyes twinkled. The mouth went wide in an enormous mirth-spread grin. The storm that broke from that apoplectic face was a tempest of laughter, broadside after broadside, jovial, tumultuous, thrusting the chin and convulsing the red-muscled throat. And something broke in Willie Updyke like a dam going out suddenly.

He was thinking of old Henry Applegate when he leaped. He swiped out madly as he sprang, and saw red. But the slashing fist missed the jaw, nipping only one of those bud-like little ears, and the storm was on him in hurricane fury, bowling him over backward, thundering as it rushed, driving him back stupefied and appalled before a dazzling aerial display of light. Blades of light. His own, and Grunner's big ivory-handled blade. *Ziff! Swish!* Hiss of shiny steel, keen-edged, murderous. Lightning that would abolish what it touched.

He wanted to charge, but his legs carried him back, and Grunner came at him eagerly, making quick, agile cuts with his monstrous blade. Willie Updyke fled around the barber chair in which Luke Adams was cuddled, head in arms, and for a while it was ring-around-the-rosy, Grunner after him and the room like a merry-go-round, voices screaming, shadows going forty ways in whirling smoke.

Grunner got him in the cheek the third time around. Grunner was squalling, "I'm going to kill you, Villie! I'm going to kill you!" The gash down his face only numbed him, and Willie spun, striking out. A band of scarlet appeared as if by magic on Grunner's roaring chest, and he screeched and whisked his blade at Grunner again. *Zaff!* The wall behind Grunner, then, was striped like the barber pole out in front; Willie fled in horror from that streaming jaw. Around the front chair. Around the back chair. Dodging, ducking, reeling and stumbling to escape that crimson face, that horrible persecuting crimson face.

It came after him. Followed him into corners. Back and across the floor. His left arm felt gone at the shoulder, and his right sleeve fluttered in scarlet rags. There was a terrible moment when they were on opposite sides of a chair, dodging left, right, left, right, like people trying to avoid bumping each other. The air was alive with razors; everywhere he turned to duck there was that big ivory-handled blade, biting at his ears, nipping his wrists and elbows, trying to get his head. Everywhere he turned there was Grunner's face, Grunner's savage eyes, Grunner's squalling jaws.

Somehow he fought back, stroke for stroke. Laid open the big man's bandaged palm. Breath sobbing, heart bursting with strain, fought his way out of corners and around chairs, fending that deadly razor, staving off certain execution. Grunner's razor didn't bring him down. The floor did. A place where the linoleum was slippery. He shrieked as his heels went out from under him. Shrieked and shot headlong into the shelf of tonic bottles where he struck at Grunner's reflection in the mirror; went down plunging.

Everything came down on top of him. Plaster from the ceiling. Grunner. The shelf in crashing rainbows of colored bottles. Cyclone of shaving mugs, talcum, scalp elixir, mange cure. In nightmare terror he grabbed to save himself; dropped his razor; caught a bottle in his out-thrown hand. Red fingers clamped on his throat as he fell, and he corkscrewed desperately, fighting in the grip of death, hitting at a razor with a bottle. Meant for his own neck, the flashing blade cut the bottle's. The quinine tonic was luck. Glass exploded and liquid flew. Blinded, Grunner rolled backward with an elbow across his eyes.

Willie Updyke couldn't remember how it ended. Somehow his razor was in his hand again, and he was mowing the air around him with wild, uncontrollable strokes. He couldn't see Grunner. There was a sickening perfume of tonic and bay rum; his eyes were shut, and he was seeing old Henry Applegate stretched out in Seymore's undertaking parlor.

When he opened his eyes the air seemed filled with rubies.

NOBODY in the chair-line moved. Nobody on the floor moved either. Nothing moved except the silent red tide creeping sluggishly toward the door which was standing open to a soundless infall of snow.

Martha, sitting among the tintypes, was whispering, "Willie—Oh, my heavens—! Willie—"

Willie Updyke tried to smile, and couldn't. He knew he was dreaming a nightmare. Borne on that red tide moving toward the door there was a thousand dollar bill. The linoleum was scattered with blood and thousand dollar bills. Willie Updyke swayed; shook his head. Grunner couldn't be bleeding money—

The room tilted and wheeled at crazy angles, and Luke Adams sat up in Grunner's chair and looked at Willie and fainted again. In the barber chair near the door Medicine Joe snored, *"Ugh."*

A shadow in the snowing doorway snapped, "What the—!" and choked off; and Trooper Eddie McElroy walked in behind a pointed gun. Holding the bead on Willie, he leaned over and picked up a thousand dollar bill, making queer stifled sounds in his mouth, staring at Grunner, at Willie.

Martha cried out in a choky voice, "Don't shoot him, Eddie! Grunner was the murderer! That money was hidden behind the mirror over that shelf!"

Willie Updyke caught the arm of a barber chair and hung

on. Postmaster Crackenbush was yelling at him, "Lord-A-mighty, Willie, how did you *know?* How'd you know it couldn't be Medicine Joe? How'd you know Grunner was lying?"

He mumbled, "Knew it from the first. If th' bandit had a beard it couldn't've been Joe. Medicine Joe's an Onandaga. Can't give an Onandaga a beard. Any barber'd know that, except some foreign-born Dutchman never heard of it before. Indians," Willie Updyke finished with a swallow, *"Indians don't have beards!"*

His eyes caught hold of a sign on the barber shop's back wall; hung on, and steadied his legs.

> HAIRCUT—40¢
> SHAVE—20¢
> SHAVING THE SICK—50¢
> SHAVING THE DEAD—$1.00

Willie Updyke reached down and took a dollar out of Grunner's pocket. Then he walked with Martha Teacher from the barber shop.

IV

I WAS THE KID WITH
THE DRUM

Once I was a boy in a strange, fascinating world....

Hats off! Along the street there comes
A blare of bugles, a ruffle of drums.
—Bartlett.

CHAPTER I

THE DRUM WAS beating by itself.... To this day I can see it standing there in the corner gloom of that upstairs back bedroom, round as a cartwheel and fat as two washtubs, its varnished hull gleaming faintly in the smoky yellow light of the chimney-lamp on the dresser, its huge-bulged shadow stenciled blackly on the gray wallpaper behind it; the drumhead, enormous, moon-pale, facing the window with the gold legend: *Four Corners Military Band,* and going, *Boom! Boom! Boom, Boom, Boom, Boom—!* filling the room and the night outside with its basso bellying resonance.

And to this day the sound of a base drum—summoning smaller boys as a magnet—starts a tickle down my spine, and gives me the same scalp-sensation I had that night when, on the woodshed roof behind the Sleeper house, I spied into an upstairs window and saw a drum booming under no visible drumstick, with no Joe Sleeper, no drummer there.

You may ask what I was doing on the Sleeper woodshed to begin with, behind that somber mansion on a night so black the stars must have turned to coal.

Be reminded that a woodshed is as fair a nocturnal territory for a boy as for a cat; and when was a bass drum not a summons? The combination of the two—forbidden precinct in a place of shades, and the biggest bass drum in (as I remember it) the world—was too much for any twelve-year-old torn between

the desire to play such a drum and the ambition to be a detective.

Sousa and Sherlock Holmes—certainly my youthful predilections were satisfied that night. A drum in the corner of a dim-lit bedroom. In *that* house! Beating by itself! I can still feel the pull at the roots of my hair, the fear-ache in my throat that was like crying.

"But there's no one *playing* it!"

I remember whispering that to myself. And how the fact, given credence by my utterance, would have sent me flying had not terror held me fast on a slope of shingles, peering across a ten-foot gulf of nothingness into that vacant room where a drum, unattended, was booming. In the sticky dark, through air too tired to move after a wilting August day, the drum-beats marched away with the sluggish tread of heavy boots in tar;

and watching them come from that yellow upper window, I went clammy sick.

The window was up a scant ten inches, but between blind and sill I could see quite enough. A bony iron bedpost. White china pitcher on wash-stand. Joe's band uniform, empty of Joe, limp on its wall hook under the girl-with-parasol calendar from Clapp's Store. All as I had viewed it on previous occasions of espionage, except—except the kitchen chair in which Joe would sit while practicing, mid-floor, big drum clamped between big knees—the chair that night was tilted against the hall door which was closed, the drum was booming in its corner, and there was no sign of Joe or his masterful drumstick anywhere.

They had to be there! I craned until I could see the area of carpet before the drum. Joe wasn't on the floor, as I had imagined he might be. The dresser-glass mirrored the outside corner of the room. Nobody there. A window at the side was open a little, letting the sound out that way. I could see the curtains stirring there as if at the passage of each big-bellied, tramping vibration. *Boom! Boom! Boom, Boom, Boom—!* My hair stayed up. Drums in ordinary houses don't play by themselves. And that drum was.

BUT THEN the Sleeper house was no ordinary house. Not unless a great rambling place that seemed always to have the moon in its cupola, the lower quarters darkened, a bandman upstairs and heaven-knew-what *downstairs*, could be called ordinary. At the time I would have said there were a hundred rooms, although, as seen back through the stingy glasses of maturity, there may have been seventeen. Which still would have made it catacombish in a village of our size, what with most of the rooms closed against former extravagance, chinks of light leaking through a mystery of shutters to make eerie the thickets of hollyhock and lilac screening the foundations, and a headless iron coach dog guarding the gate. Weed-grown side-yards flourish as jungles in the summer months. About a hundred yards from the right-hand wing where a garden path skulked through a forest of five droopy-limbed locust trees there was the latticework wreckage of a summerhouse. And there was an old apple orchard at the back where, they say, Carrie Sleeper's father once cut his own throat with a pruning knife— and didn't die by it, but went around afterward, to the day of his natural death, speechless and stark-eyed, his Adam's apple collared by a great red scar puckered by little crow's-feet along the edges where Doc Trosch had sewed the skin together. But that was before my time; my first memory of the house was a blue light and a smell.

The front hall always had a blue light in it, not from the bronze lamp hanging as a great mouldy fruit above the staircase, but from the colored-glass window in the tall, black, thin front-door. Mildew was the smell. I can recall, sent there on an errand when my mother was alive, handing a parcel of some sort through that door to Mrs. Sleeper, and getting, instead of a hoped-for penny, that stale breath—like old wet books. And what a funny, stringy, unappetizing little woman Mrs. Sleeper was, like a herring dried with the eyes in, even to a five-year-old who didn't, as he did at twelve, knew all about Spiritualism and "voices" and the meetings held by the Circle.

There were five in that esoteric Circle. Mayzie Peterson, Elmira Johns, Floss Watters, Hesther Boul and that old Mrs. McKenzie who used to rock all evening on her veranda muttering to herself. Together with Mrs. Sleeper they would sit in her parlor, listening to the voices of the Departed and things like that, all holding hands with the lights out. It was said Mrs. Sleeper's dead father often returned and prowled the house with his hemstitched throat, talking just as loud as he used to before he incised his gullet with his own hand. There were secret rappings and bells sometimes. Mrs. Sleeper was a medium. She went into trances and could see in the dark.

Of the latter phenomenon I had convincing proof, for how else could she have seen Wart Baxter and me on the woodshed roof that time in July? "Mrs. Sleeper," my father had said, "complains about certain boys climbing on that woodshed back of her house. Keep off it, son." He'd had a glint in his eye when he said it, the same glint I'd seen him use on poachers and vagrants, and I knew the tone of mandate. Father happened to be sheriff in Four Corners, and it was his conviction that the sheriff's son, "same as a minister's," must show an exemplary respect for rectitude, law and order.

But a chance to investigate the Spirit World made it a hard dictum, and the added attraction of Joe Sleeper's drum was too much to resist.

"There's just two things in the world that big dumbhead loves," I'd heard it said. "One is that drum of his, and the other—"

His wife, of course. It never occurred to me to wonder about the pause. Why Joe Sleeper, wide, burly, stove-cheeked Joe, with

his little match-head eyes, his furtive whisky bottle and his big
bass drum, ever married the dried-up female gnome who was
his wife was something a boy never wondered about. I had
heard talk about "for her money," which meant nothing to me,
and "because he had to," which meant less. That Joe and his
drum should be resident of that dank house on Locust Street
seemed as natural to me as the sunrise over Appleby's barn, the
river bending blue across the Valley five miles to the west, the
recurrent seasons and the Labor-Day Fair over at Brockton. I
never saw him, either, as a silent, uncommunicative man. Not
with that big bass drum on his stomach.

How he could play that homely instrument! The hours he
spent practicing on it! Not just whacking it as other bass drum-
mers do, but making an art of drumming, juggling the sticks,
drubbing the thing and making it sound almost alive. Today
most boys are discussing short-wave reception and airplane
motors. In those days the ambition of a boy (in Four Corners
at least) was to help Joe carry that big drum in a concert or a
parade. Joe was pretty careful about who assisted him with the
drum, and he never missed a parade or concert as long as he
lived in our village. Dumb? It was his wife's lips that were sealed
on secrets.

It was not until a long time afterwards that I couldn't understand why he married the woman.

But looking back, I can see there may have been a time when
Carrie's hair was not iron gray and her face oyster-colored.
When she wasn't shrunken and corded with hands like bird's
feet and eyes that saw beyond the Veil. When, to the roving
blink of on itinerant bandsman just home from the Spanish-
American War, she may have been small and soft-haired and
frilly, all pins and lace and "hoity-toity," which was my father's
expression for Myrtle Dockstader, whatever that meant.

Myrtle Dockstader. I knew her as having some part in the
aura of strangeness emanating from that house on Locust Street,
although she lived in old Weingarth cottage up Blackberry Hill,
about a mile by road from the Sleeper place, half mile crosslots

by the back path through the orchard, by the path that skirted the ruined summerhouse. My father's dislike for Myrtle was as incomprehensible to me as various comments let fall by other villagers within my hearing. Her name linked with "such goin's on" or "it's a brazen shame." Her departing footfalls occasioning such remarks as, "Says she's goin' to call on *Mrs.* Sleeper. That's a good one, that is." Selma Barrows shaking her head. "My land!" inexplicably outraged. Or Mordecai Sailor's wife growling, too incomprehensibly, "It's funny Mrs. Sleeper can't *see*—*!*"

I LIKED Myrtle Dockstader. Like Mrs. Sleeper she was small and unfathomable, but she made me think of a doll and was decidedly not unappetizing. She could play the mandolin and sing, *Yoohoo, Yoohoo, Yoohoo, Ain'tcha Coming Out Tonight* and *Take Me To Saint Looey, Looey.* She was the Candy Lady.

Chocolate fudge. Taffy. Caramels. Fondant. Merely to meet her on Locust Street at a moment when it was otherwise deserted was to assure myself a miraculous windfall of sweets. Somehow this delectable fortune came after an evening, dimly recalled now, when the Four Corners hopefuls were playing Cowboy'n Indian, and I, dragooned as an Apache brave and reluctantly stalking General Custer in the Black Hills of the Sleeper sideyard, came suddenly on Joe Sleeper and Myrtle Dockstader in the summerhouse. In the dimness I thought her Mrs. Sleeper until I became aware of flurried ribbons and pink dress. Then Joe, it seems to me, was glowering over me with an upraised bottle. Myrtle, breathlessly patting her hair, darted from shadow with a, "No, Joe, no—!" It was pretty frightening, especially when Mrs. Sleeper appeared, a black specter at a corner wing of the house. It was all right, though, I ducked like sixty, and when I turned to look back, there were Mrs. Sleeper and Joe and Myrtle all going into the Sleeper kitchen: Myrtle laughing and telling Mrs. Sleeper how well she looked. If Myrtle's generous philanthropy came as an aftermath, what boy could look a gift gumdrop in the teeth?

So I knew Myrtle was maligned, particularly by that, "It's

funny Mrs. Sleeper can't *see*—!" What couldn't she see, that woman with the X-ray eyes? And why shouldn't Myrtle call there; wasn't Mrs. Sleeper always flitting up the path to Mrytle's? Myrtle didn't belong to the Circle, but I'd heard her say she was interested in spirits and the like. Lem Renfew once said maybe the spirits she was interested in were a different kind, the kind Joe was interested in, the kind you could put down your throat. And that was funny, because the only thing I'd ever seen Joe put down his throat was whisky.

I thought Joe was maligned, too. Even if he did sit up there in his bedroom practicing on his drum at all hours. Wasn't he the best drummer our band ever had, the way he could toss the drumsticks up in the air and catch them and cross his arms over the drum and just make it bellow? Nobody looked as fine in a uniform, red and green, and who could blame him for locking himself in his upstairs room and booming his head off while the Circle held hands in the parlor? Nights of the meetings he'd play the drum so loud you could hear it all across Blue Valley—especially on August nights when the air was still and hot.

Boom! Boom! Boom, Boom, Boom—!

It was quite beyond my capacity for law and order—hearing the drum that evening, and reminded, too (as if I could have forgotten it!) how Joe had promised me a nickel and the glory of helping him carry his drum in the massed bands contest at Brockton Fair on Labor Day, coming Saturday. I was aloft on the Sleeper woodshed as if whisked there by Sinbad's carpet.

Didn't I regret my transgression when I saw the drum in Joe's bedroom was beating by itself! To say my retreat was precipitous is to minimize the celerity of its execution. Heart pounding louder than ten drums, I started across the sideyard lickety-split, and would have abandoned music and mystery in record time had I not fallen headlong across a ladder lying in wait in the grass. But I knew who had tripped me! When I sat up, panic-choked, Mrs. Sleeper's old father had my throat in his dead, invisible hands.

One other phantasm I remember, something that wasn't fright-inspired illusion. In the roof of locust leaves above my head a bough was swishing. Not a breath of wind, and that bough whisking in the blackness overhead as if the tree were waving one of its limbs, keeping time with the drum in the house. *Swish—Swish—Swish, Swish, Swish—!* I fled.

I imagine it was the first time in history the beat of a bass drum had chased a small boy home. I could hear it after me all the way down Locust Street and up Valley Street and over my back fence and into my own upstairs bedroom. Mrs. Sleeper's dead father was as close at heel, oyster-faced and crimson-throated, snatching at my shirt tail with gauzy hands; and only as I put this down it comes to me that hands might indeed have captured my throat there in the Sleeper sideyard; choked the life out of me. Mortal hands. Murderer's hands.

But I got my head under my pillow, and the next thing I knew it was morning and loud voices were competing on our front porch and Joe Sleeper was telling Father his wife had been out all night and hadn't returned.

"**WHAT** time you say your wife left the house, Joe?" Father's voice hadn't sounded at all worried about it. Then.

Joe's voice didn't sound worried, either, only louder than usual, half indignant, half amused. "Around half past eight, it was. Just put on her hat and come up to my room—I was practicin' the drum—and said she was goin' out."

"Didn't say where at all?"

"That's what I can't exactly remember—whether she said she was goin' to *pay* a call or she'd *had* a call. You know about how Carrie has *calls*—and—well, it's darn funny nobody's seen her or got the slightest—"

"Ask over at old Mrs. McKenzie's, Joe? She might be—"

"Just come from there, Sheriff. Mrs. McKenzie ain't seen her."

"How about Myrtle Dockstader? Myrtle might've taken sick or something, and Mrs. Sleeper stayed up on Blackberry Hill."

"Myrtle ain't to home; she told Mrs. Sleeper yest'day morning she was goin' away to visit somewhere over Labor Day—relatives somewhere I guess—said she was takin' the nine-twelve train last night, so Carrie wouldn't hardly be up there. If only she didn't talk like she sometimes does—"

I heard Father say, "Don't know as I'd let that bother me, Joe; all women get notions at times, 'specially when it comes to anything to do with religion. Carrie Sleeper's more religious than most, it's likely, and she sees a lot of meaning in dreams and that kind of thing."

Joe said, "Only you know how she talks about maybe she can go to the Other Side an' come back. What she calls Transferrin' herself to th' Hereafter—"

"Sure." There was reassurance in the way my father pulled out the word. "Sure, Joe. And if I was you, I'd drive up to the cemetery, maybe. Might find she'd transferred herself up there to spend the night at her father's grave or something like that. You'll see."

On my way downstairs I heard Joe's voice flatted in complaint, "Yeah, but I'd just as soon she wouldn't go playin'. These spooky capers kinda leave you up in the air, and I had to fix my own breakfast. Anyhow, I thought I'd ask, case you see anybody's seen her. I sent Norman up to Mayzie Peterson's to ask and— oh, an' tell that boy of yours if he wants to carry th' drum for me at th' Fair tomorrow night he'll hafta fetch a ride somebody else, I won't have no room in my buggy what with th' drum."

"I'll tell him. Wait. You might ask th' kids around, Joe, they generally know a lot of what's going on in th' village. Maybe some of the youngsters playin' Stillwaters or something around here last night saw Carrie on the street." Father lifted his voice. "Hi, son! Come down to the porch a minute; Joe Sleeper'd like to see you!"

I walked out guiltily, the door-screen printed on my nose. Father gave me a narrow look for listening, and, "Well?"

"I didn't see nothin'," I said sullenly.

JOE SLEEPER was looking at me. He was big and round-shouldered on the porch steps, kind of rumpled and sheepish and puzzled looking. He said, "Don't forget tomorrow night, Bud, you want to help me carry the drum."

I could only eye him, swallowing and wordless, while Father's stare became impatient. "What's the matter with you this morning, son? Let's see your tongue…. Well, tuck in your shirt. Now then, you or the other boys didn't happen to see Mrs. Sleeper any time last evening?"

"I didn't see nothin'," I insisted.

Joe scrubbed his forehead with a blue polka-dot bandanna and said he'd be on his way after some ice; it was going to be another scorcher; reminding me of the woodshed where he kept his ice in sawdust. He was off down the street, large and distracted, leaving a faint flavor of whisky in the sunlight where he'd been standing. Small and distracted, I wanted to cry after him to tell him I'd changed my mind about carrying his drum at the Brockton Fair, but Father said something about "into the house quick" and "oatmeal," and opportunity was lost. Father came in to join me with his second cup of coffee, as was his custom; yawned, unfolded the morning paper, but then instead of reading, sat staring thoughtfully across the dining room into the door of his office. I could see into the office—the brown rolltop desk with its fascinating pigeon-holes, Father's sheriff's badge on the blotter, his gun-holster hooked negligently over the back of the swivel chair.

The hall clock went *ding-ding-ding* six times. Sunshine made bright patterns on windows cooled by honeysuckle, and everything was as usual that morning, yet everything was alien. Presently, feeling my cheeks heating again, I knew Father's eyes were on me. My interest in oatmeal must have seemed extraordinary.

"Sure you weren't on Locust Street last night around eight-thirty, son?"

I said I was sure. Truthfully. For I hadn't been there until nine showed on the yellow face of Town-Hall clock, and then not on Locust Street, unfortunately, but atop the forbidden woodshed. And perhaps not even there. In the clement clarity of morning, the night's ghosts had started to dissolve, and I was not certain on waking that it hadn't been a dream. How could a drum beat by itself? But then how did I tear my stockings and get a painful purple bark across each shin? I looked up.

"Pop, do you believe in Spiritualism?"

"Why?"

It was like him. Father never answered a question without first wanting to know why you'd asked it. It occurs to me now that it may have afforded him a moment's advantage to consider his reply, to decide whether he could answer with authenticity or say honestly, as he often did, that he didn't know.

"I just asked, that's all. On account of Joe saying Mrs. Sleeper was out all night and she believing in spirits and—and all."

Oddly, he was paying no attention, but frowning at the window where the sunshine had brightened in the honeysuckle. He said, as if thinking aloud, "Funny if she came out her front door nobody'd see her, a hot night like last, everybody sitting out on their lawns…. No, I don't know anything about things like that, things that *might* be, and you just can't say you don't believe 'em. Myself, I don't believe in souls you can see floating around, in ghosts and miracles or anything contrary to nature, although there may be spirits. I mean, I think there's an answer for everything. A natural answer. Take Mrs. Sleeper leaving the house and nobody seeing her—that doesn't mean she was all the sudden invisible. Either she sneaked out on purpose, say, or she just went out th' back door." He put aside his coffee cup. "Want to walk over to th' Sleeper place a minute? Something I wanted to ask Joe."

I gulped, "Wuh-walk over to the Sleepers? I c-can't—!"

"What *is* the matter with you this morning?"

"There ain't nothing the matter with me."

"There's plenty the matter with your English, young man."

"That's why I wanted to stay home and read up," I said hopefully. "I'm reading *The Little Shepherd of Kingdom Come*. There isn't nothing the matter with me, Father."

"What that boy needs," Minerva's voice loafed out of the kitchen, "is summo' that now Castoria. He sho' look this mo'nin' kinda peeked."

My recovery to robust health was instantaneous; I was at his heels through the door, first to reach the gate, relieved to note Father hadn't slipped his badge into his hip pocket, which meant our errand was unimportant and we wouldn't be long. And so I was party to the finding of the bullet, the second enigma witnessed in what afterward was to be headlined in village gossip as "The Sleeper Horror."

CHAPTER II

NOT THAT I was ever actively involved, save for the one episode of dreadful cooperation at the last, a collusion in which I was not morally responsible. To the end I was hardly more than an innocent bystander—how was I to imagine the impossible seance between bedroom and drum, glimpsed at a moment of trespassing, might have anything to do with a homicide. Had I been directly questioned on the point I certainly would have spoken. As it was, I wanted badly to relieve myself of the haunting subject, but the thought of Father's exactions of law-enforcement, no less heavy on my britches than on the collars of adult malefactors, stayed my tongue. And no direct question was put to me. Everything to the last (even for Father) was under the surface. Hints. Indirections. A feeling. Nothing you could put your finger on. Something that might mean everything or nothing, like the finding of the little brass shell-case in the ferns.

Surely the morning's face was virtuous—fresh green and yellow—front-yards, sidewalks and maples clean-laundered by a nocturnal rain. Leopard Smith reared a spotted head above his woodpile and hailed, "Hi!" shying a chip. Then he saw my father and ducked. I felt better. At the corner, Locust Street was so complacent that I started whistling manfully when we reached the Sleeper's gate. Father halted on the brick walk to appraise the house, and I saw the front door was open, only the faintest suggestion of blue light in the hall.

"Used to be quite a place when old Mr. Brackett was alive and things were solid at the bank. But it ought still to be worth plenty as property goes." He took down his pipe. "Hello…Joe… Anybody home?"

A gray cat looked out of the door. Nothing else stirred.

"Guess he's not back yet with the ice," Father said. "Come on, son, we'll wait around at the back."

I walked pretty close to Father; in that gray house morning had not quite dispelled all shadows. When we rounded the wing and came to the back I sped a furtive glance upward to the bedroom windows. Both windows were wide, and of last night's witchery the house gave no sign. Father tapped his pipe-stem on his teeth, speculating on the kitchen door; then I saw him studying the path that led off under the locust trees to the green-hidden summerhouse.

"Looks like someone might've walked down there."

He moved down the path at a saunter, and my heart gave a skip. Father was no mean woodsman—he had hunted in a day when deer, foxes and beaver were no rarity in Blue Valley—and he had a keen, uncanny vision when it came to tracks. What if he saw my own heels recorded around here?

"Too muddy," he shook his head, "to tell much. Rain's washed out anything that was here before midnight. Someone'd been down it, though." Stooping over a bed of catnip bordering the path, he plucked a crushed sprig, squinted at it, held it out. "Know what stepped on this last night, sonny?"

I didn't. He seemed amused. "Why, I think it was some kind of skunk. Anyhow"—three paces further on, he was examining a fat clump of burdocks—"here's something. Know what this is?"

I couldn't see it at first. Then it looked like fine wisps of brown hair caught in the hooky prickers. As if a dog or a tan cat had brushed by. Father must have had eyes like microscopes.

"Jute. Off burlap," he declared. "Somebody went by draggin' a brand new gunnysack, yesterday I'd say. Probably Ed Brown bringin' Mrs. Sleeper a bag of potatoes."

THE PATH descended into quagmire of puddles which afforded Father little opportunity to play this favorite game of his, but he idled on, smiling to himself. He seemed interested in the skunk and mentioned it again. My eyes were lifted to a canopy of locust leaves, and I was uneasily recalling how I'd heard them swishing in last night's dark as if the tree had been alive. I was praying at the same time that Father wouldn't come on my track; certain the prayer would not be answered. In those days I thought Father easily on a level with Sherlock Holmes, not to mention Theodore Roosevelt. I'll never forget the disappointment when, old with sixteen years, I first realized his deductive powers, dependent often on such chance leads of fate as the jump of a squirrel, were hardly up to those of the infallible Holmes, or his career quite the equal of T.R.'s. And how pleased I am today to think my adolescent cynicism unjustified, for Holmes was only a fiction, and surely somewhere in T.R.'s life fortuitous squirrels must have run across his path, even as a red one dashed into the summerhouse that morning with Mildred, our old beagle who must have followed us over to the Sleeper place, in full hue and cry, bringing us running to a fateful discovery.

Either Mildred or the squirrel must have kicked it into view on their race out the back. A brass shell-case glinting in a dark corner of the summer-house, a bright new object in that ferny recess of green light where wasps drifted and toads bounced into hiding under decayed lattice. I have not forgotten Father's eyes as they spied the discharged cartridge. First wide, then narrow as he picked it up, held it to his nostrils, sniffing.

"Forty-five." He had forgotten I was there. "Rain hasn't

washed out th' smell. Fired in th' last day or so, I'd say. Now who"—he held up the little cylinder between thumb and fore-finger, squinting distastefully—"was down here some time last evening an' shot off a revolver?"

A revolver. It sent a little tingle through me. Father hated revolvers; always the word brought to mind those rare occasions when he carried his own, phone calls late at night, excited voices in the house, a bandit, a mob, a dead man somewhere. "Rifles," he had once said to me, "are for hunting. Pistols and revolvers are made for killing men."

"How do you know it was last evening?" I had to ask.

His gaze was on the path where it bent around the foot of a locust and climbed off from Blackberry Hill through blight-ed apple trees. "Eh? Well, I don't say for certain. There was this downpour at midnight, lasted about twenty minutes. Anyone here *after* that, there'd be tracks left in th' mud, so they must've been here before. I'd time it between eight and midnight because I was across th' street all day yesterday up to eight o'clock at Ed Brown's auction—these forty-fives bang like a cannon, an' if one had been fired durin' th' day we'd have heard it at Ed's. I'd guess last evening, or it wouldn't still smell of powder."

He sniffed it again. Father had the nostrils of an Indian. But I don't suppose at the time he smelled any connection between this find and Mrs. Sleeper's reported absence; probably he was trying to remember which of his neighbors owned so powerful a firearm, and wondering the direction of the bullet shucked from the brass case. I murmured, "Gosh!" thinking of someone here in the summerhouse with a gun when I'd fled the ghostly premises. Suppose it had been Mrs. Sleeper, or—or her dead father summoned from the grave by that spectral drumming? Watching the solemnity on my father's face, I wanted to get out.

THEN all at once Joe was there, standing in the vine-arbored doorway looking at us, a shadow at the entrance of the sum-merhouse, his eyes just staring. Coolness drifted from a cake of ice that was melting, dwindling almost visibly on his shoulder, and something melted and dwindled inside of me, the way he was staring at my father's back, breathing through parted lips and not making any sound. His expression—somehow I was reminded of the time long ago when I'd come on him in this viny bower with Myrtle Dockstader. I wanted to run. Then Father, sensing his presence, wheeled around.

"What is it, Joe? Carrie—?"

He let down the ice as if it weighed a ton. "You scairt me for a minute. Seen you down here, an' thought maybe somethin' was wrong. Carrie wasn't up to the cemetery, Sheriff, an' Norman, here, says she wasn't to Mayzie Peterson's, neither."

An old Negro, as gray and shabby as a dilapidated rubber boot, shuffled from behind Joe Sleeper's bulk; stood quavering and bobbing confirmation. Besides being Minerva's father and claiming the advanced age of a hundred years, this elderly Uncle Tom sometimes roused himself from Civil War memories and did odd jobs around the neighborhood.

"—And when I see you got a burnt cartridge in your hand," Joe was continuing, "it sort of startled me. Where's it from?"

"Can't say," Father's tone was mild. "You wouldn't've been shootin' blanks around here last Fourth of July, would you? Or skunk, maybe?"

"Not me, Sheriff. I ain't got a gun even. Carrie wouldn't allow one in the house." His eyes rounded. "Judas! you don't think—"

"Don't think anything, Joe. My guess is somebody fired off a forty-five down here in the summerhouse sometime last night before midnight. Didn't hear any shooting around here, did you, Joe?"

"Me? I was in th' house up there in my room practicin' on th' drum right from suppertime to twelve. I wouldn't of heard nothin'."

Father nodded, "I heard you drummin'." And I opened my mouth to speak, and couldn't. Norman's eyes were an interruption. Fixed on the little cylinder in Father's palm, the pupils grew, the whites went big as butterplates. "Yassuh, yassuh What was summun doin' here with a gun? I knowed I shouldn't come by this summa'house las' night—it's sho' haunted!"

Father's glance swerved. "What time you by here, Norman?"

"Mistah Joe'd done ask me bring him some beer from th' poolroom, an' I stop by with it jus' befo' midnight. Mistah Joe come down from where he been drummin' upstairs, ask me if I seen Mrs. Sleeper. Nossuh, I don' see nobody. Ain' nobody in this summa'house when I pass it, either, 'cause I stop in to light my lantern jus' as it comes on rain." His eyes roamed. "Yo' don' 'spect it was one of Mrs. Sleeper's ghosts—?"

Joe said uneasily, "I don't like it, either, an' I sure wish Carrie'd turn up, with Labor Day comin' tomorrow an' me havin' to play in the band an' all. We got to win that prize, Sheriff, an' if Carrie ain't there—"

Father said something hopeful—nobody could be missing very long in a town the size of Four Corners—and told Joe if anything came up to let him know. I had to run to keep pace with him on the path back to the house and around to the front gate. I couldn't look back at Joe or Norman, and on the front walk I couldn't contain it. "Father, might there really be spirits in the Sleepers' house? I mean, ones that *aren't* natural—like—like miracles?"

"What do you mean, like miracles?"

I said, "Well—like Mrs. Sleeper all the sudden walking out an' not seen." (What I meant was, like Joe saying he'd been practicing the drum all evening when it was beating by itself the time I saw it.) "I mean—like what Mrs. Sleeper calls being Transferred to the Hereafter?"

"There might be something in it," Father nodded abstractedly.

But I didn't think he was thinking about what I meant. His eyes were clouded, and his hand was jiggling in in the pocket where he'd put the brass shell-case. The remainder of that fast walk home he was thoughtfully silent; slamming into the house with a, "Wait!" he went straight to his office, and when he came back out to the porch, I saw him slipping his badge into his hip pocket.

WHY Father insisted I drive with him up to Myrtle Dockstader's I don't know, unless he planned to keep me handy for a probable tire-change. Demountable rims and six-ply treads were still in the future, along with teletype, short-wave radio and streamlined district attorneys. Police work in those days was as slow and devious as our progress up Blackberry Hill.

The cottage on Blackberry Hill was closed and in prim order, and Father merely tried the doors and returned to the car. Descending the hill, he kept his thoughts to himself. Similarly I reserved mine, although I was as ready as our front tires to burst. This internal pressure was not lessened when Father steered down Main Street to Clapp's Store, where he engaged Thunder, our storekeeper, in low-voiced exchange of enigmas over behind the coffee mill. In the background, eating raisins, I caught fragments of what seemed dark conversation.

"—Carrie Sleeper? Sure, Sheriff, everybody knows—Joe was askin'. All th' women folk in here talkin' about it. Can't imagine—"

"But what I want to know, Thun—you sell the only forty-five ammunition in th' county. Recall sellin' anyone around here that size shell?"

"Don't carry 'em no more. No call. Long time ago maybe—"

"Wouldn't have been to Mrs. Sleeper or Joe—?"

"But I've heard Joe say he never had a gun in th' house."

"—or Myrtle Dockstader, by any chance?"

"Her? Not's I recall. Say, Sheriff, you don't think—"

"Suicides," Father said, emphasizing the word, "are common enough. Anyone can borrow a pistol or get one easy by mail order. If you—"

"Mail order! Why, say, come to think of it he was lookin' at the Sears-Roebuck catalogue right here in the store last Sat'day. Joe. Recollect he stood over ther browsin' in th' catalogue, and

I see him all the sudden tear out an order blank an' go out kind of excited. Came back after while sayin' he'd forgot his errand, and bought some chicken feed, three big balls of twine an' a box of fruit-jar rubbers. I wanted to ask him what he'd got out of the catalogue—"

In memory I see Father thumbing through that encyclopedic work, hustling bashfully over pages of ladies in long underwear, hounding through chapters of furniture and farm machinery, coming at long last to the page from which an order blank had been torn. The subject? Band instruments. A double spread of wonderfully lithographed tubas, clarinets, French horns, drums, their manifold parts and accessories. I remember it clearly, for there I saw for the first time that strange new beast, the saxophone. If Father had expected something more revelatory than a *menu* of brasses and woodwinds, his features disclosed no chagrin. He glanced over the prospectus idly, but I knew his eyes were taking a mental photograph of that colorful page.

"Uh-huh. And just forget our talk here, will you, Thun?"

On the walk to the Post Office he told Elmira Johns that no, he hadn't heard if Mrs. Sleeper was back yet, but he'd bet she'd be at the King's Daughters social that night. I didn't hear what he asked of Postmaster Crackenbush. The mousy face at the window said, "Yes, sir, he did get one yesterday morning. About so high, so wide. Kind of heavy, too."

Father mimicked the pantomime of a package eight by ten, smiling soberly. I know now he was thinking, "About right for a Colt, only you wouldn't order one on a blank out of band instruments." I know, too, the finding of the .45 shell in the Sleeper summerhouse, coincident with Mrs. Sleeper's unaccountable truancy, had, as he would have phrased it, "stuck in his crop." And I know that Myrtle Dockstader "off visitin' somewhere," had occurred to him as the possible x in an old, old geometric equation.

BUT I didn't know it then. All I knew was that the cloud of mystery brooding over the house on Locust Street had darkened, spread, and was reaching out across the village as a shadow moving with the sun. Something was up. In the hot noon wind that rustled dryness across the Valley's sweep, you could hear voices. "She ain't back yet."—"Left about eight-thirty las' night, Joe says."—"Looked everywhere."—"Not that I take any stock in them spooks."—"That worried he's down to th' Tavern a-drink-in'."—"—called to her Beyond."—"Elmira Johns says—"—"Selma Barrows says—"—"Mrs. McKenzie says—"

Voices. Mortal but hardly less mysterious than the dark-room whispers reported as heard by the Circle (a very knowing, and frightened little Circle, by this time) during meetings at the Sleeper house. "Always said she was waitin' for a *call*—!"—"Didn't she tell Floss Watters how sometime she was goin' to visit the *Other* Side?"—"Mind over matter, she'd say. *Think* you're somewhere, and you're there."—"Power, that's what she had. Once told us she'd do somethin' to prove it to Joe."

Also there was the back-fence voice of Mrs. Mordecai Sailor echoing into our dining room from three lots away. "Worried, is he? Well, why don't he go up an' cry on that *hussy's* shoulder, then. As if *he'd* care if poor Carrie went to her Beyond to visit her father or for good! Not with all that prop'ty he'd have to live on with that *hussy*—*!*"

"Father, what's a hussy?"

"Eh? What one woman always thinks another is. Don't bother me today, boy."

He pushed away his plate; went into his office where I could hear him cranking the phone, then speaking to Lawyer Brickle. "You look up what I asked you? Yes… You say she changed it lately at his request…. You don't know what's in it…. Think the house worth that much?… Yes, confidential." The receiver clucked on its hook; Father came out frowning. "Don't do any extra talkin' today, will you, son? And I'd just as soon you kept our business around town this morning under your hat."

There again, where through an opening in conversation I

might have rid myself of my ill-gotten knowledge, I was silenced. And I wanted desperately to add my own voice to the medley, for if there were numerous skeptics like Mrs. Mordecai Sailor and Undertaker Seymore ("You don't hear no voices in *my* parlor!") and the afternoon crowd on Town Hall steps ("Tell you, boys, this spirit stuff is a lotta josh, an' if she's dropped outa sight it's likely down somebody's well!")—if there were many who disbelieved in occult manifestations, I was not one of them.

How I could have told them at Town Hall when Fire Chief Ganning said to Mule Lickette, "We gotta do something; find Mrs. Sleeper. If Joe don't play in the band we'll lose."

Mule said: "He's a whiz on that drum, all right, practicin' all the time like he was last night." I could have laughed. Or cried. Someone on the crowd's fringe said Joe didn't do so bad with Myrtle Dockstader, either; and Father, elbowing up just then, ordered me home.

He was late for supper, and I started a tasteless, unhappy meal in the kitchen with Minerva and Mildred, planning to bolt for Wart Baxter's as soon as it was over. Wart would be surprised when I offered him the honor of being drummer's assistant at tomorrow night's Fair. Father came in just as the lamps were lighting, irritably opening a wilted collar and muttering Shakespeare. "What fools we mortals be!"

Reinforced by Minerva's cooking, I summoned resolve. "Father—?"

"Children, unless they have something to say, should be seen and not heard. Got anything to say?"

Unfairly challenged, I muttered a sullen, "Wouldn't tell you if I did!" and was ordered to bed without dessert. But presently he was coming up to my tower cell with vanilla ice cream to murmur, "It's a pretty hot night, son, and maybe I was kind of short." He sat by companionably to watch me eat, and then he was talking about George Washington who was crossing the Delaware at the foot of my bed, laying quiet emphasis on our First President's fine command of Truth. How then could

I admit my delinquency, or refuse his offer to let me drive with him over to the King's Daughters social and maybe afterward down to watch the 9:12 come in?

No, Mrs. Sleeper was not among the good ladies on the First Church lawn, and the depot was for me the last episode of that baffling day. Four Corners was a flagstop for the Albany-bound 9:12, and anyone boarding the express at our platform would certainly be locally remarked. Cut-plug in cheek, Dunk Weatherbell leaned on a Well's-Fargo truck and considered Father's question drowsily.

"Who got aboard her last night? Well, Sheriff, a couple of these now traveling salesmen, I think, yes, and Myrtle Dockstader come in yest'day afternoon an' bought a ticket f' Albany now, but I didn't *see* who got aboard, count of when th' train pulled in I went down th' tracks to talk with the engineer. No, I didn't really see—"

Then the train conductor, new to the line by a week, was in some asperity at Father's interruption of schedule until he saw the badge.

"Yes, some passengers got on last night…. Dark and I didn't pay attention to their faces…. Yes, a woman…. Well, folks in *this* burg might take her for good looking—"

Father was so savage at that parting comment that he stood with clenched fists, glaring at the dwindling lights of the parlor car; and I dared not open my lips all the way home.

It was a guilt-haunted, ghost-ridden twelve-year-old who was afraid to turn out the lamp after creeping into bed that night. Over the Fire House the Four Corners Military Band was triumphing through a final rehearsal, and like a baneful dead-march sounded the percussion, a somber undertone throbbing through the strains of Sousa.

Boom! Boom! Boom, Boom, Boom!

The drum weighed heavily on me as I lay there wide-eyed and listening. Tomorrow, I promised myself, I would transfer this burden to the unsuspecting shoulders of Wart Baxter. Relieved by the thought, I fell asleep—and put off what I should have done today.

THAT was Labor Day Eve. At ten-thirty that night, The Fire House rehearsal over, the musicians gone home and the village asleep, Floss Watters sat bolt upright in bed, shrieking to her bust and that someone was groaning under their window. Jacob Watters, decidedly an Unbeliever, heard it too. Armed with poker and flatiron, and cloaking the embarrassment of a night-shirt with his Sunday derby, Jacob foot-raced around the prem-ises and stubbed his toe on Mrs. Sleeper's cat. Mrs. Sleeper's cat was as dead as a taxidermist's dummy, pained surprise on its feline face.

At ten forty-five Elmira Johns, roused by hysteria and shout-ing across the street at the Watters domicile, looked out of her bedroom window and saw "clear as anything" a white wraith go fluttering across her yard and over her back fence. The ter-rified Elmira did some fluttering, herself—out through her front door to the street where she fainted with drama, with grace, and without her teeth under a street-lamp.

At eleven P.M., four blocks away, Mrs. McKenzie was awak-ened by a cold wind blowing across her forehead and a faint tapping at her bedroom shutters. Every hair of her wig stood on end as her eyes beheld candlelight sprinkling at her through the shutters from the outside. Slowly the shutters whispered open. Framed in the sill was a white, shapeless figure, with eyes like winter moons in a blank and featureless face, a hand that was nothing but a blur holding up the pallid candle. According to Mrs. McKenzie, this visitation was not unlike a melting tombstone (whatever that would be like), and its voice was three octaves lower than a sermon in a sepulchre. "I am Carrie Sleeper. I am with my father. I am happy." Contented or not, the ap-paritional presence failed to cheer Mrs. McKenzie. Mrs. McK-enzie went, "Waaaaah!" and her visitor went away, leaving a faint odor of dead lilacs in its wake.

At eleven-ten Father left our house with his holster on his

shoulder, only to find that his frightened neighbors had tram-
pled out all hope of tracks or reason; that at least a dozen villagers—including Micah Appleby, deaf as a post—had heard
unearthly groans, and a dozen more—including Aunt Sue
Dingerman, blind in one eye—had seen Mrs. Sleeper's spirit
afoot in the dark.

By eleven-thirty at least forty people were gathered before
the house on Locust Street trying to hear what my father was
saying to Joe Sleeper on that dim veranda. Opening the door
to Father's summons, Joe had peered out in nightshirted bewilderment. No, he hadn't heard a word from Carrie yet. Yes,
he'd come straight home from the Fire House with his drum,
gone right to bed. Heard anything around the house? Not a
sound. The cat? Why, he'd put it out when he went to bed.

Father was still questioning Joe when midnight arrived, and
with it, to nightcap the climax, Norman. I would like to have
seen the faces of that crowd when Norman appeared. Particularly Joe's. They said the aged Negro came hollering down
Locust Street at cannon-ball speed, his complexion white as
any Aryan's, wailing, "Lawd forgive me! Lawd forgive me!" His
travail he knew was a divine punishment for chicken-stealing.
He'd been on his way to exploit an especially fat coop of Buff
Orpingtons when it happened. Not only had he collided full-tilt
into Mrs. Sleeper's ghost in the dark, but she'd grabbed him by
the arm. When? Not ten minutes ago? Where? Up there on
Blackberry Hill—!

I slept through it all. Home in bed, dreaming a huge bass
drum was chasing me on and on across a black world while I
cried for help and couldn't lift my voice above its hollow
booming, I missed a nightmare of actuality. Led by Father and
Joe, men with shotguns, lanterns and dogs were combing the
slopes of Blackberry Hill for Mrs. Sleeper while I dreamed she
was feeding me candy in her unlighted parlor, only it wasn't her
parlor but the summerhouse; Myrtle Dockstader was there, and
Joe glowered over me with an up-raised drumstick. At four of
the morning the hunting party was still thrashing through the

brier above the Sleeper orchard, and it was sunrise when my father came on a broken scarecrow at the hillcrest, glared down at the uprooted straw man and snapped, "Great heaven! let's go home—"

But he must have been pretty worried as he tramped down-hill with Joe and the others in the early mist. It was all right to say, "Bosh!" to ghosts, but the fact remained that Mrs. Sleeper was still missing. Minerva told me he kept turning his head and looking off toward Myrtle Dockstader's cottage, distant on the slope. Frowning.

Minerva saw it all. Up all night with her rabbit's foot, she had followed the wild-ghost-chase from the dead cat on Watters' lawn to that fantastic disclosure unveiled by the dawn on Blackberry Hill. But she never told me about it until after-noon, when it was too late—

CHAPTER III

LABOR DAY. IT was that morning when I first perceived the holiday for some of us—those who stand and wait, as well as those who serve—was not inappropriately named.

There was Joe Sleeper. Every time I saw him that morning (twice, anyway) he was sweating homeward under a fresh cake of ice—not the only load he was carrying, either, judging by the wobble to his knees. Wanted it, he told the boys at the Fire House, to cool his beer. Joe was drowning his anxieties, every-body could see that.

There was Father. Beginning the day at seven with a call to the telegraph office, he was gone the remainder of the forenoon with his two deputies, only heaven and Minerva knew where. It is not to be supposed my diligent parent expended all or even most of his time on the Sleeper business; I have set down here only his measures taken to satisfy himself there wasn't any case—to the end he believed Mrs. Sleeper would "turn up"— meanwhile there were routine duties to occupy him, the jail to be inspected, the new traffic laws to be enforced, that sort of detail. But I did pry out of Minerva that Father had telegraphed a state-wide alarm for Mrs. Sleeper, and that his deputies were searching the Valley as far as the river five miles away.

Gossip worked overtime that morning, back fences bearing the brunt, but there was a heavy strain, too, on rockers, screen doors and palmleaf fans. Opinion had now divided into two general camps: the mystics and the materialists.

And I? A devout mystic, I walked the way of the Transgressor, burdened as only Atlas must have been under the World. But I doubt if anyone who noticed me that day, wan, leaden-footed and hangdog, recognized my load as a drum. That drum was on my mind like a ten-ton weight, an oppression I could neither drop nor escape, and as the red sun toiled up into noon my burden swelled with the thermometer.

Unaware of *last* night's jabberwock doings, I had stuffed down a hearty breakfast and started at once for Wart Baxter's, thinking to put my troubles on his shoulders. It was a hot, red morning that cooled nine degrees when Wart's mother told me he'd gone fishing with his uncles. Then Leopard Smith had a sprained ankle; Tommy Brown's mother wouldn't let him go to Brockton, and when Mumbly-Peg Peterson refused my generous proposal without thanks, slamming the door in my face, I began to sense something vital had gone wrong in Four Corners.

What had happened? There was something in the air. Something in the way men were congregated in little groups on street corners. Something tense and electric that had nothing to do with the normally unusual atmosphere of a holiday. Everything was queer. Why, for instance, when it was Mrs. Sleeper who'd disappeared, did Myrtle Dockstader's name keep echoing out of the conversations which made unquiet little pools of talk up and down Main Street? Why was there a crowd at Floss Watters' bungalow, at Elmira Johns', at old Mrs. McKenzie's? It all had to do with that old house on Locust Street, I knew, and that bogey drum was somehow in the middle of it.

My desperation grew. One after another my boyhood cronies

refused my offer to let them carry the drum in my stead, whereas a week ago they would have fought for the chance. Did they know about it, too? They knew *something!*

In torment, I slunk along Main Street, breathing an atmosphere that might have wafted straight from Mrs. Sleeper's parlor. A last miserable hope—the hope that Joe might resign from the band at a time of domestic misfortune—was extinguished at the Fire House where I found the big drummer in conference with his fellow musicians.

"Don't worry, Joe." That was the Fire Department, a majority membership in the band. "Keep your shirt on, fella. Didn't th' sheriff say she'd turn up?"

Joe was mopping his forehead unhappily. "Can't help but worry, folks talkin' like they are. And all them goin's-on last night—"

"Well, you know how that turned out," he was reminded. "An' take it easy on th' bottle, Joe, you can't let us down tonight after how we been rehearsin' all year, an' got new uniforms and all. You and your drum's th' whole band. Where'd we get another drummer if you drop out?"

"Drop out?" You can see Joe's haggard glance looking around in worried appeal. "I couldn't do that, could I? People'd say I was afraid to appear in public. Yeah—I'll play all right, all right. Th' sheriff's kid, he's gonna help me carry th' drum—"

I backed out of the Fire House, tongue-tied. Like fun, I was going to carry that bass drum! Not me! There was only one thing left for me to do, and I was on my way to do it. Tell Father what I'd seen from that forbidden woodshed roof; take my licking, but make a clean breast of it.

But the Destiny that shapes our ends (be it with razor straps or bullets) defeated my good intention. Father, that sultry noon, wasn't home. Blurting into his office, I stopped up short; breath congealed in my lungs. The holster was gone from his swivel chair, and there on the desk instead of his badge, I saw the little brass shell he'd picked up in the Sleeper summerhouse and, stiff on a piece of newspaper, Mrs. Sleeper's dead cat.

My yell brought Minerva, and when she told me of last night's witcheries, rolling her eyeballs in a way that would have frightened even the Fox Sisters, I would have traded my partnership with Joe Sleeper for a dozen razor-strappings.

"We find this ole scarecrow knocked flat on top that hill," Minerva described with gestures, "an' yo' daddy tell us all g'wan home to baid, th' ain't no ghosts at all. Huh."

SHE KNEW better, and so did I. I had no appetite for dinner *that* noon. Mistaking my pallor for illness, Minerva dosed me with Castoria. It gave me an excuse to lock myself in my room, but it didn't take the taste of apprehension out of my mouth. *The Little Shepherd Of Kingdom Come* couldn't banish the specter of a drum beating by itself in yellow lamplight while locust leaves waved time in the dark.

So Mrs. Sleeper's spirit had come back last night? Now I knew the meaning of Joe's cryptic reference to "all them goin's-on," the reason for the tension on Main Street, the crowds at Floss Watters' gungalow and old Mrs. McKenzie's. Father was off somewhere looking for "natural" answers, but I *knew*.

I remember pacing up and down the floor, groaning, "If a drum can beat by itself, anything can happen!" Mildred came waddling upstairs to pace with me. But a locked door and a dog couldn't keep Mrs. Sleeper out of my room that afternoon, any more than her disappearance could absent her from our village.

I fancy Mrs. Sleeper was present in Four Corners that day as she hadn't been in a lifetime of visible occupancy. She was there. From one end of the Valley to the other. In the dust and sunlight on Main Street even as she entered my room on the rustle of a window curtain, the lengthening shadows of waning day. Mrs. Sleeper! Mrs. Sleeper! Actually I began to hear her name. Joe's name, too! Myrtle Dockstader's! My father's! All at once Mildred was barking, there was a sound of running footsteps, uproar in the street outside, tramping on our porch, someone shouting for the sheriff.

I don't know which frightened me more—the clock striking six in the twilight of the hall, or the throng of people streaming past our house and swerving like a flood into Locust Street. When I opened the door there was no one on the porch, and all of Four Corners was going by.

How do mobs start? What unseen messenger gathers and gives them momentum? Everyone was shouting to everyone else, "What's happened? What's happened, now?" and all I know is that I was drawn into that running stream like a water-drop adding its mite to an irresistible current broken from an exploded dam. But I suppose village gossip, working overtime like chemicals in that day's heat, had started the thing. Some-one's talk had set off a fuse. Lord knows, it couldn't have been mine; but Norman, who had seen things, was neither deaf nor blind, and certainly not dumb, and the old Negro was foremost in that race. So were Mrs. Mordecai Sailor and Banker Barrows and Ma Peterson and a lot of tall people.

We poured into Locust Street where I didn't want to go, and into the Sleeper gate where I tried to turn back and was swept along in the rush. Then, arrived at the front steps of that out-sprawled, shadow-winged mansion, the crowd stopped, stood uncertainly, as if it didn't quite know what to do. Joe's horse and buggy were waiting at the side—I recall a sickening sensation when I realized he must have harnessed up for the drive to the Brockton fairgrounds—otherwise the house, already purple-gloomed in dusk, appeared deserted.

IT WAS Mrs. Mordecai Sailor who braved the veranda's dimness to knock on that forbidding front door. A hush of lavender gloaming spread over the waiting crowd, and it seemed a long time before Joe was there. I can see him yet as he opened that thin, black door and bulked elephantine in the narrow frame, stood rooted and glaring at the population massed below the veranda. Red and green, gilt-frogged, his new band uniform contrasted strangely to the somber background of the hall. He was carrying his instrument, and the bass drum, enormously aloft, was like some overpowering menace crouching on his shoulder, and there was that blue hall-light of Spiritualism on his face.

"Watcher want—?" I don't know why the thick slur to his words made me think the big man suddenly afraid.

"Where's Mrs. Sleeper?" The discordant tenor in the voice of the woman on the veranda told me she was afraid, too. Afraid and determined. "We want to know where's Mrs. Sleeper?"

"How should I know?" Joe lumbered out on the veranda, shifting the weight of the drum. "How sh'd I know where—ain't I been lookin' for two whole days?" His voice rose off key as his eyes roamed the crowd. "Watcher want here, anyhow? I got to get over to th' Brockton Fair by seven, an' th' band's gone already in Spud Myers's truck. I'm in a hurry—I—what'd make you think I knew where my wife was—ain't I been looking everywhere?"

"Maybe you ain't been looking close enough to home!"

"Close enough to home!" He swayed back under his drum; glared at Mrs. Mordecai Sailor as if she'd hit him. Everything was queerer than ever, and I couldn't understand any of this. People shoving around me couldn't seem to understand it, either—there was a lot of pushing and craning and exclaiming—Joe looming there on his doormat, flabbergasted. "Watcher mean, close enough to home?"

"In th' house!" That was Norman's cry, squealing up in the twilight. "Right there in th' house, Mistah Joe! I *seen* her!"

"I seen her, too! We both seen her! Her face," Mrs. Mordecai Sailor shrilled. "It looked right out of the window at me! She was behind the curtains, there, and her face looked right out the window!"

An audible indrawing of fifty breaths as the tall woman turned, pointed at the vine-screened wing that stretched off in darkness beyond the veranda. People recoiling around me. Someone gasping, "Holy gee!" Joe's face imbecilic, bawling, "There ain't nobody in th' house—I just been upstairs gettin' into my uniform—there ain't been a soul in them front rooms for ten years!"

Mrs. Mordecai Sailor yelled, "She was so! I seen her!"

And then my father's voice was crackling from somewhere behind me, an interruption as loud as gunshots. "Seen who! What's going on here? Why ain't all you people over to th' fairgrounds watchin' Lincoln Beachey fly that airship?"

WE HADN'T heard his car skid up to the curb. Confusion grew as he came elbowing into the yard, ramming his way through the press. He never looked at me as he went by. His badge was on his lapel; his eyes were glinting and his jaw looked good and mad. Father feared nothing. He looked like an irritated bulldog glaring between the big man and the tall woman there on the veranda. "What's the matter here? Who seen who?"

Joe said hoarsely, "They all come rantin' into my yard just now. Mrs. Sailor says she seen my wife's face at the window."

"Behind the curtains there," Mrs. Sailor cried. "Pale as a sheet."

"Fiddlesticks!" Father swerved angrily. "Has everybody in this village lost their heads! Running around last night like a lot of kids on Hallowe'en! A cat howls under Floss Watters's window and she thinks it's Mrs. Sleeper's ghost. Huh! Wasn't anything but Mrs. Sleeper's cat with a belly full of rat poison some of you neighbors must've left around. Sure, I found enough arsenic in it to bring howls out of a tiger—"

"I tell you, Sheriff Whittier, I saw Mrs. Sleeper's face! Not half an hour ago! I and Norman were going by on the street with th' laundry—"

"Laundry! Well, that's what Elmira Johns saw last night. Nothin' but a white sheet off th' wash line that I found blowin' on her back fence—"

Mrs. Mordecai Sailor screeched, "This wasn't any sheet. It was just a half hour ago an' daylight. Carrie Sleeper's face looked out from behind them curtains and—"

"As for old Mrs. McKenzie," Father roared on implacably,

"everybody knows she's been seein' visions and spooks ever since her grandfather's Clydesdale kicked her in the head when she was eight. I'm not surprised at old Norman, here, thinkin' it's a spook when he's got chicken-stealing on his conscience an' runs smack into Farmer Lickette's new scarecrow up there in th' dark on Blackberry Hill. But I'm surprised at you, Mrs. Sailor. Thought you was Congregationalist. You turned Spiritualist, too? Believin' in ghosts?"

"I didn't say it was a ghost!"

Father's jaw wasn't the only one that dropped. A stagger shook through the crowd, and Joe Sleeper, stooped under the big drum, gave a sort of whinny.

"I'd know Carrie Sleeper's face anywhere. It didn't look natural, no sir, not a bit natural behind them curtains, but it was her as sure as I'm standin' here. Th' curtains moved, too." Mrs. Mordecai Sailor's voice rose falsetto. "I don't hold no truck with this spirit business. I know Carrie Sleeper when I see her. She's right here in this house, and that big drunken husband of hers knows she is." Finger quivering heavenward, the woman faced that stupefied assemblage of neighbors with all the flaming indignation of an evangelist summoning the Judgments of the Lord to fall on secret Sin. "Heaven knows why she's bein' kept in there, but as a good neighbor of Carrie Sleeper's I think we ought to find out. I tell you people, there's somethin' terrible going on in this house!"

Father spun at the big man. "Joe, is your wife in the house?"

He shook his head soddenly. "Ain't no one in there, Sheriff."

"Her spirit!" The wail issued from Elmira Johns somewhere in the audience. "It's her astral spirit!"

"Spirit or not," Mrs. Mordecai Sailor cried, "her face was behind them curtains for a minute! On my soul, it did look more dead than alive. She's in the house, I tell you. Joe Sleeper's keepin' here there!"

"Why would I keep her in? Why?"

"Why don't the law ask that?" pointing militantly at Father.

"How about that bullet Norman says was found in th' summerhouse? Why don't the law do something! Maybe Carrie was shot! If that drunken husband of hers—"

Father cut in savagely, "Maybe you'd like to be sheriff, woman! That bullet was fired Thursday evening when Joe was in th' house practicin' his drum. Heard him playin' it, myself."

"Well, Myrtle Dockstader wasn't playin' any drum. Where's *she* gone to? Wouldn't put it past her to shoot somebody. Nor Joe to keep his wife in th' house—wounded, maybe—not wantin' any charges brought against that hussy!"

I COULDN'T understand the effect of that speech, any more than I could fathom its meaning. All around me faces went askew. Mouths flew open. Eyes fixed on Joe Sleeper, everybody gave a sort of silent yell. Sweat shone on Joe's face like a coating of pale blue varnish, and, balancing the huge drum with one hand, he had to catch the veranda-rail with the other for support. He swayed at the woman beside Father. He squalled, "That's a lie!"

Mrs. Mordecai Sailor screeched: "Why don't you let us search your house then?"

"Nobody's going to search anything without proper warrant!" Father declared thunderously. He rounded on Joe, his glare blazing. "Only let me tell you, Sleeper, if she's in there, if you're trying to put over some—"

"Go in! Search th' house! Let 'em all search th' house!' The tormented man bellowed like an Alderney bull. "I been over it from top to bottom! There ain't nobody there, an' I ain't got time to go lookin' for Carrie anymore tonight. Glad to have anyone search th' place! Let th' whole town look if it wants to!"

And the whole town looked, I do believe. Every citizen of Four Corners, with the small exception of the band on its way to Brockton in Spud Myers's truck, must have been there by that time. Drum aloft, Joe came blundering down to the brick walk; everybody drew back to let him by; then everybody was rubbernecking, shoving toward the veranda to see what Father would do, and when Father stamped into that moony hall, everybody streamed in after him.

Houses absorb the personalities of their owners, and the personality of that house clings to my skin to this day. Wallpaper peeling from damp plaster. Tarnished woodwork. Gray corridors where hatracks stood like skeletons. Unused rooms that made tombs for dead furniture, the broken walnut and plush of a forgotten era, moldered carpets, mildewed drapes. In that abode of intellectual decline and wealth impoverished, the clamor of two hundred people trampling upstairs, downstairs, opening doors, poking into alcoves made the tumult of an invasion in an Egyptian crypt. All my neighbors became ghosts in that stale gloom. Lost in foggy nightmare, I don't know how I reached Father's side.

Alone, he was standing in what had seen better days as a music room—(I mark how curiously the thread of music weaves through this discordant drama!)—a dim little chamber recessed off an alcove of that unused front wing. There was no music, now, in that cobwebby dimness where a decayed grand piano had lost most of its yellow teeth—and none on my father's face. Wrath on his forehead frightened me. Almost as much as the object of his rage.

He was glaring at something on the wall, and I didn't see it as a picture at first. Last ray of sunset, a blade of crimson light penetrated ragged lace on the front window; gave the thing life. Carrie Sleeper looked down at me from a funeral wreath on the wall. The eyes followed my rush to the safety of Father's hand.

Then, rescued by his grip, I saw more clearly. Life-sized photographic portrait. Framed in an oval of tarnished gilt leaves, one of those crayon-tinted family-album horrors you still see in photographers' windows in the Italian quarter. Even then it was old fashioned and stary-eyed. Feathers of color in the cheeks looked like make-up on a corpse. The veil over the hair was a shroud. Portrait of Carrie Sleeper as a bride!

Father did a queer thing. Dropping my hand, he darted across the floor, turned the picture to look at the back of the frame, wheeled toward the window infuriated. The light was going, and feet were pounding above the ceiling, and I knew I ought to tell him about what I'd seen in that upstairs back bedroom, but his face scared speech from my tongue. Something rushed by the window outside. Fast spatter of hoofbeats, wheels screeching on the driveway's turn, scattering gravel. Twilight faded with this sound. Father started for the door, swerved, handcuffed my wrist with iron fingers.

"Come on! That's Joe! We got to get going or you'll be late to carry th' drum for him at th' Fair—"

I choked out: "But I don't want to carry that old drum at the Fair. I don't want—"

Dreadful that Father, of all people, should have shut the last door on my escape. "But I want you to! Don't ask questions, boy! We'll drive along after him to Brockton, it'll likely be dark time we get there, and I want you to stick close to Joe on the fairgrounds, understand? Don't let him out of your sight! After th' concert I'll come for you!"

In the hall he shouted at someone to keep on with the search for Mrs. Sleeper. I tried to break his grip on the veranda. "Father, I *can't*—"

"What's the matter? Always wanted to be a drummer, didn't you? Or a detective? Here's a chance for both. You stick in that parade with him, sonny. Anyone in the crowd tries to jump on him, or he walks off by himself somewheres, you run let me know. Tell you all about it afterward," he said grimly. "But this much I'll tell you. Someone's holding somethin' back about this Sleeper business. Someone's holding somethin' back, and it's going to be just too bad when I find out who and what it is!"

Tell him then? Tell him *I* was the one who was holding something back? He was cranking the car. It was as if that cat of Mrs. Sleeper's had got my tongue. We were driving furiously down Locust Street. Father's eyes glinted at the windshield as I'd seen them glint at the countenances of criminals. The car shot past the jail. Maybe I'd get the electric chair.

Hardly a spider's-wink later I was trudging across the fairgrounds, heavy laden, to the tune of *There'll Be A Hot Time In The Old Town Tonight.*

CHAPTER IV

THEN—SPIRITS, AVAUNT! EXUENT ghosts and phantoms! What astral conjuration could live in that carnival of bunting, Cracker Jack and flagging torchlight. What specter could keep step with our gaily bedecked company swinging its way through dust and rocket-glare and applause to the frolicsome tempo of that brassy American classic? *Dah—Dah—Dah—dada, da da, da da, Daah—!* Let 'er go, boys! Give it all we got! We'll show that one-horse outfit from Midvale, that high-falutin' Brockton bunch, a *real* band!

Nothing ghostly cloaking the figure of our high-stepping, baton-twirling drum major, hardly recognizable in his jaunty bearskin shako as our expert mortician, Mr. Theodore Seymore. No spooks in the blaring trombones and blazing French horns of our transformed Fire Department, going full-lunged in the van of our four silver-toned cornets. Where could an apparition find sanctuary in the doughty-cheeked tuba of Mr. Eric Hausle, *Fresh Meats*, or the double-belled euphonium of Dr. Clyde Wilbur, *Veterinary*, or Algebra-teacher Getz's indomitable fife. And only the timidest of banshees hiding (and hastily squelched) in Blacksmith Dan Buchanan's piccolo.

"Hit it, fellas!"

Starting from the main gate, we advanced down the field with the circumstance of a showboat, the tootling ebullience of a steam calliope. Ghosts? On that holiday midway where people were massed blurs cheering under strung constellations of Japanese lanterns? Goblins around that grandstand where faces, rosy in torch-glow, were polished apples banked on bright shelves and the mayor of Brockton, big as a pumpkin, stood up to salute us in review? Confetti drifted while straw hats, tonic bottles, fans, handkerchiefs waved and fluttered, catching time to our brazen minstrelsy, urging us on. Applause threatened to drown us out. "Lookit 'em come!"—"Here's th' Four Corners boys!"—" 'Raaay!" Flourish from our band leader signaling a prouder air. *Flimflam* of tympani to strike her up.

Rum-bum—Rum-bum—rrrrrrrrrr—Rum-bum—!

Yes we'll rally round the flag, boys; we'll rally once again—

You can hear it blaring forth in the lusty fortissimo of martial fervor. See the swinging shoulders of the bandmen, their nodding parade caps, puffing cheeks, rhythmic strides. Lights as well as harmonics splashing out of belled instruments. Music-notes almost visibly pouring out of pumped horns, flowing across the parade lines to start them jigging, shaking torch-light in the foliage of park trees, flooding the summer dark beyond with brilliant sound—

But, then, in memory I have weird associations. Play Sousa, and I see, instead of gala fairgrounds, an old dark mansion screened with rumors and boscage; instead of festive grandstand, a rotted summerhouse, a figure towering from gloom while a breathless little woman in pink gasps, "No, Joe, no—!" and later my father standing there with a glint of brass on bis palm. Play *A Hot Time In The Old Town*, and I see a silent little woman in black whose eyes always stared at séance; I see her vanishing as a shadow in pitchy night; I see a burly man sweating under cakes of ice, a village whispering, a closed cottage on a hill. Play a bass drum—I see a small boy leaden-footed at the tail of a bright parade, hair disheveled, lips open, shoulders stooped, one stocking down—a boy whose eyes roam wildly through confetti and carnival glow, as scared and miserable as if bringing up the rear of a dirge-paced *marche funébre*—

Ghosts? But I think no one who saw the Four-Corners Military Band go into action that night would have believed its drummer's assistant in an escort of haunts. I think not one of those cheering onlookers saw, somewhere in the tinted dust behind me, walking lightfoot and invisible, Mrs. Sleeper's dead father with his floating hair and fish-scale eyes and pruned throat. There was no other witness to the spook of Mrs. Sleeper, who flitted at my elbow, cat at heel; no onlooker who suspected I bore on my shoulders such a spine-chilling phantasm as no swooning swami ever dreamed.

The night was sultry. Heat flowed from blazing kerosene flares along the sidelines; tunic collars wilted ahead of me; sweat spilled down my nose. And my hands were chill! My fingers gripped one of those metal crossbars that clamp the rims to the drumheads, and that bar was like the handle of a refrigerator. Actually that drum was cold! As cold and heavy (I remember shuddering off the thought) as a coffin.

Why shouldn't it be heavy? Wasn't it the biggest bass drum in ten counties, metal-bound, vellum-headed, round as a tallow vat? And who ever heard of a cold bass drum? But who ever heard of a bass drum in the corner of a lamp-lit bedroom beating by itself? No, it wasn't that memory which was shivering my fingerbones. The cold crawled up my wrists; came through the drum's hull into my back.

"It don't sound *right*—"

THAT was Joe. His voice husked through a fragment of piccolo solo just as I turned my head to see if he felt it, too. He looked as if he felt something. Plodding at the rear of the band—the drum between us, we were like some fabulous four-legged animal driving a herd of blaring bipeds—he was glaring around the curving drum-rim in a way that put mice in my hair. So close behind me, he seemed as huge as Jack's giant; I might have been supporting his stomach. His fists were like swinging hams, he was beating his great belly with monster turkey-legs, and his face was glazed shiny greenish like the metal inside a salmon can.

"Does it sound right to you, kid?"

It didn't. It wasn't booming as I'd heard it before. Its tone was more a thump, like stamping on wooden planks.

He began to twist feverishly at nickel screws along the rim, pounding with one hand, twisting with the other. Looking back at him, I almost stumbled, and he shouted at me to keep in step. Keep in step? I wanted to run. I wanted to break ranks and bolt. Get back down the field to the ticket gate where Father waited near the hitching line of carriages and parked automobiles. At that moment of stumbling, Joe's face had gone ptomaine blue. Worse than it was on the veranda when Mrs. Sailor had said that about Myrtle Dockstader. Worse than when, unloading his buggy at the fairgrounds gate, he'd turned to look at Father's car driving in, and almost dropped the drum to the ground.

What I wouldn't have given, then, to be carrying Tom Lickette's snare drum, five paces to the left! Why hadn't I sold my soul to the devil for a fife or one of those smaller instruments advertised in the Sears-Roebuck catalogue? All the specters of Tophet trooped behind me after that—!

But the remainder of that jamboree I recall only as one remembers the fitful hallucinations of fever. Red lights tossing through dust. Smell of hay and popcorn. Blur of faces, toy balloons, trombones, flags. Bright saturnalia in which my knees were turning to water, my hands seemed icy, the drum was back-breaking, colder and colder, and I was hunting my father's Stetson in the crowd's wall, frantic because I couldn't find it.

I don't know how long it lasted. Moments were years that night, and the music went round and round. Ahead of us marched the Hazelton Ladies' Band in Scotch kilts, and the Midvale Memorials in scarlet. Behind us came the Valley Spring B.P.O.E. and the Brockton Fife and Drum Corps. Far down the field musicians paraded and wheeled under plumage like flocks of glittering birds, and our leader's baton exhorted us to outdo all competition. But my heart wasn't in it. I was too sick to care if the Brockton Corps would win because of bells on their drums, or the Midvale Memorials because they were the only band boasting a glockenspiel.

But, then, if we didn't have a glockenspiel or drum-jells we had a bass drum matched by no other drum on earth! And the champion drummer of all time! No onlooker who saw Joe Sleeper's performance on our second swing past the grandstand could have denied that. His exhibition with the drumsticks that night makes Four Corners conversation to this day. He swung them. Spun them like a juggler. Tossed them high and caught them in mid air. He twirled them over his cap; whirled them beside his ears. Crossing his arms over the drum's shell, he pounded with a fury to split the vellum heads.

"Hey, there's Joe Sleeper."—"You show 'em, Joe!"—"Attaboy, Joe!"

Applause breaking through the crashing chords of brass inspired him to superhuman virtuosity. Sweat washed down his face like quicksilver, spiraled off his wrists. Between slow-timed beats I could hear his lungs chugging. Head arched back, cap awry, he kept hitching his leather shoulder strap to balance the drum's weight; had to keep tightening the rim-screws. But he never missed a beat when we crashed *John Brown's Body Lies A-moldering in the Grave.*

Ironical we should have ended on that, and lucky for me! John Brown's soul (and other souls!) might have gone marching on, but I was finished. My hands were like ice, the pervading chill of that drum had reached my heart when Band-Leader Seymore blew his whistle to steer our little company right oblique across the field. Horns blurted a final fanfare. Joe swung his inspired arms in a last windmill flourish, we were through.

IT WAS over. A shade of apple trees at field's end remote from the crowd. Musicians shrugging off their instruments, mopping flushed faces, spitting. Seymore calling out, "Great work, boys. Th' mayor'll announce th' prize any minute now." A thick voice behind me panting, "Pit it down over *there!*" and I, half paralyzed, easing the freezy monster of wood and steel-bound vellum to the grass beside a shadowy tree.

Panic-addled, I stood staring at the ground, trying to decide which way to run. It was dark there under the trees. Like standing in the wings of a theater and looking out on a lighted stage. Night made a wall behind us, and bandmen stood in silhouette between me and the light. I wanted to get away from there.

"Did it sound all *right?*"

Joe leaning over me, both hands gripping the grounded drum, body sagging, all in. I could hear his breathing. Flesh was strained across his temples where a shaft of torch-glow coming across the field made a crimson streak. His eyes were bright slits, two points of narcotic shine. Voice raw and intended only for my hearing.

"Did it sound all right to you, kid?"

I stood swallowing, unable to answer. Wanting to run. How could I tell him that from now on in my haunted world nothing would ever *be* all right, much less sound it?

Somewhere miles away a band was finishing up with (of all selections) *My Wife's Gone to the Country,* Joe's gaze was on me in a sort of desperation.

"—or did it sound kind of—kind of dead?"

It was theatrical how, at the moment of those words, lightning branched across the sky like a sudden crack in the shell of a black Easter egg. How dust scurried over the field and all the flags in the grandstand whipped alive; tremored lights fluttered the edges of outer darkness, people caught at their hats. Then it wasn't thunder that saved me from an answer, but cheering.

Rataplan of clapping hands. Thousand-tongued applause. Joe Sleeper! Joe Sleeper! The name tossed up on waves of sound as I'd heard his wife's name echoing into my room that afternoon. The big drummer lifting his head, staring drunkenly at the bright-hazed bedlam. Band-leader Seymore darting at us from the crowd's fringe, grabbing Joe's arm.

"You done it! We won! We won the prize and you done it for us—th' mayor just announced it was your drumming—brilliant performance, he called it—played soft enough so's they could hear the other instruments—Hey, Joe!—They want you to take a bow—in th' grandstand!"

"In the—! I can't take th' drum up there!"

"Leave it. You got to go! Mayor of Brockton wants to meet you!"

"I can't leave th' drum—!"

"Th' kid'll watch it for you. Won't you, kid?"

I gasped. "Wa—?"

"Hurry up, Joe!" Men jostled around us, pummeling him. "Get out there!"—"They're calling for you!"—"Take a bow!"—"Mayor wants you!"

"Watch that drum, kid! Don't let nobody fool with it! Don't touch it!"

Touch it? I saw him swept out from under the tree, rushed off on the shoulders of the band. Shadows closed around me, and I was alone in a nest of musical instruments—in the dark—left behind. The more left behind for all those people yelling with their backs turned on me a hundred feet away. The lonelier for the presence of that drum at my side. In the dimness it seemed to grow. I could see the thin shine of its cleats. Its great pale face was watching me. Hypnotizing me. Touch it? That crouching beast? Wild horses couldn't have made me put a finger on it—

Bumm—!

Distinctly, without warning, as if thumped by ghostly knuckles that drum let out sound.

Joe's cry echoed back, "Hey, keep away from that drum—!" But *I* hadn't touched it—no living thing had touched it—hands frozen behind my back, eyes mesmerized, I'd been posed beyond reach, atrophied.

I broke that atrophy with the violence of spontaneous combustion. Theodore Seymour, who saw me, told me I came over that clutter of band instruments and out from under that tree like a rabbit flushed from cover by a hundred dogs. I don't know. A trombone had me by the foot, and I thought it was Mrs. Sleeper's dead father, the way he'd tripped me that time in the Sleeper sideyard under that bough-waving locust tree. My throat was stuffed with dry cotton, and I was screaming, "Father! Father! Father!" hardly raising more than a squeak. Joe tumbled down from the platform of shoulders with, "Wait—Bud—!" and I went under his legs like an arrow going under the Colossus of Rhodes. Wait for nothing! Red and green bandmen spilled sideward as I fought a path through to the bright lights. Then I was battling through a multitude of arms, elbows, tall solid backs; kicking and clawing; tunneling into a wall of angry grown-ups who bawled, "Here now!" and "What the devil!" catching at me with big hands.

I BATTED off the hands and tipped over a fat man. Some woman cried, "It's Sheriff Whittier's boy!" Shapes lunged and threshed around me in front of the grandstand, shouting, "What's the matter?" and everybody was trying to hold me back, and then all at once I was lost in a great swirling sea of umbrellas, shadows dodging every which-way, women's voices shrilling, lights going out, the sky coming down like a roof of black glass.

It was as if all the awfulness of the last two days were whooping down. Skirts, bonnets, waste paper, coattails whirled by me in a slash of water. Mud flew up. Lanterns were snuffed. My panic made this a hurricane. Butting, pounding, I was spun off into the maelstrom like a fly drowning in a mill-race.

"Father—! Father—!"

A dripping black phantom loomed in front of me; caught me in streaming, tree-limbed arms. I scratched and bit.

And then it was ended. Undramatically there wasn't even a storm. Just that one brief gust of rain, fatal to tissue-paper lanterns and rude to ladies' hats. The spatter expiring to a drizzle that dissolved all further festivities, cleared the fairgrounds, started carriages, bicycles, automobiles and people going home as they always go. The arms enfolding me were my father's, and the lights of our car, glimmering at me through mist, made the dawn that is always brighter for the dark.

"What is it, son? Cheat Lord! why all the stampede—?"

"Mrs. Sleeper!" I sobbed from under the haven of his water proof coat. "Her dead spirit—over there beyond th' grand-stand—played Joe's drum! Muh-Mrs. Sleeper—come back from the Hereafter—!"

"Mrs. Sleeper—Hereafter—hell!" my father said acridly, swearing for the first time within my hearing. "Mrs. Sleeper's spirit fiddlesticks! Come on, boy, we'll be the last ones out of here. There's been entirely too much nonsense about Mrs. Sleeper!"

Only when we were in the car, a lantern on the seat between us, and Father groping for his keys, I saw his eyes were grinning.

"Don't know, though, as I can blame you, son. I guess we both been fools about Mrs. Sleeper."

His chuckle forgave me as he pulled a damp flimsy of yellow paper from his pocket, spread it on his knee. I can still see that telegram as it came to light, the opening sentence that leapt up off the paper to lithograph itself on my memory until I die. Addressed to Father, a message from the Albany police.

> MRS. SLEEPER PICKED UP IN ALBANY EIGHT O'CLOCK THIS EVENING SAYS CAME HERE TO CARRY ON WORK AS SPIRIT MEDIUM.

The police had subjected her to questioning on this subject (I could imagine her replies as spirited) and there was quite a report. She had run away from Four Corners, she said, because she couldn't stand her husband's drumming any more. He was dissolute, and insisted on playing his bass drum at ungodly hours. She didn't see why there should be a fuss at her leaving him. Thursday afternoon a friend, Myrtle Dockstader, had invited her to call that evening to discuss Psychic Phenomena. Her husband, after supper, had settled down for a noisy evening at drumming, and she had decided that night would be as good to leave him as any. Without bothering to pack a bag, she had gone up to Myrtle Dockstader's on Blackberry Hill and told Myrtle she was leaving Four Corners for good; asked Myrtle to convey this news to her husband as she didn't have the heart to tell him, herself, and barely had time to cut crosslots and catch the 9:12 train. She was determined never to return to Four Corners; her spirit moved her to larger fields of endeavor; her husband was welcome to the house and property.

The Albany police concluded with the opinion that the woman was crazy as a hoot-owl, but they could find no cause for detaining her; and Father finished reading with a snort.

"Albany! Helluva Hereafter to transfer to, if you ask me. But I suppose Joe—" He broke off; shrugged. Then with a headshake, "Myrtle never told him. Prob'ly just had time to catch th' train that night, herself. If that smart conductor had noticed two women got on, I'd have saved Joe a heap of botherment. Anyhow, Mrs. Sleeper will have to tell him, now. I wired th' police to make her send him a telegram."

As we bumped out onto the river road we passed Joe. In the dark and drizzle, last on the field, the big drummer with his instrument on his shoulder was stumbling toward his unlighted buggy.

CHAPTER V

I HAVE OFTEN wondered what would have happened if I'd kept my mouth shut. Would Joe, receiving his wife's telegram at home, with time to think about it, have asked her back; promised quieter evenings? Would he have lived alone in that haunted house, bound in dreadful companionship with that drum? Would Myrtle Dockstader have returned from her weekend holiday as she did? Would she have stayed forever with "relatives"; been forgotten?

But I couldn't stand it.

All the way across the Valley I sat twisting and squirming, lips compressed, cheeks blown and eyes averted, as sick as if I'd eaten a hundred green apples, while Father lectured on how everything had an answer, usually a pretty ordinary one, "like this business about Mrs. Sleeper," and nothing was "contrary to nature."

"Folks ain't satisfied with sunrise and sunset for miracles—they got to have vanishing-acts and tricks, like God was a cheap magician. If they *do* see spooks, it's generally something they've eaten, or like that portrait photograph Mrs. Sailor an' Norman must've seen in that front room from th' street when sunlight touched th' backwall or th' curtains blew aside or somethin'!"

Then, with the village street-lamps showing as fuzzy yellow balls in the mist ahead, with Lem's Garage at the right and Clapp's Store going by, with Mildred's bark floating from somewhere at the familiar racket of our car, the whole mess blurted up, undigestible.

"But there *are* ghosts—! I heard them! I heard them in that old house the night Mrs. Sleeper went away! I was on the woodshed! Father, I—I was on the Sleepers' woodshed that night!"

His smile came sideward. "I was wondering when you were going to tell me. I knew all the time."

"You knew—?"

He grinned, honking the horn at old Mrs. McKenzie's pet pig. "Remember I found a track in some catnip? Had those triangle pegs I put in your heels on it. I said it was a kind of skunk—"

"But the drum up in Joe's bedroom," I wailed, too convulsed to realize my father's grin an award for honesty and no dire punishment was forthcoming. "The drum up in Joe's bedroom! It was beating by itself!'

"What's that, son?" indifferently. Then, "*What—?*"

"The locust trees were keeping time with it, and Joe wasn't anywhere in the bedroom at all, and I could see it through an open window—Joe's drum—beating by itself!"

It came up. All of it. Everything from the fall I'd taken across the ladder in the weeds, certain I'd be pushed by Mrs. Sleeper's dismal father, to the drum emitting a phantom boom in the lonely grove beyond the grandstand. Father said, "Lord!" at the beginning; "The devil!" when I told about the drum being cold; then, "Good-God-I-wonder!" all run together like that.

He swung the car so suddenly it almost went through Mayzie Peterson's fence. We shot back for Brockton. I was too scared for tears. Five black wet miles and five black wet minutes farther I was too scared for anything when Father jammed the brakes and we skidded up to Joe Sleeper's horse and buggy standing at the bridgehead by the river.

THE SCENE, grotesque, irrational, was in the vaporised setting of a dream. Pattern of the bridge-rail white against swimming void. Sound of water rushing below. Light refracted from wet timberwork and puddles. Everything dripping. Joe's horse giving off a rank steam, and Joe, himself, steaming there by the buggy-step, his big drum beside him in the mud. Back toward our lights as we drove up, he was stooped over the drum, intent on working the rim-screws. Father leaned out to stare at Joe, and I wouldn't have recognized the big drummer when he flung around at us, blinking into the mist-smudged focus of the car-lamps. In the drizzle his face looked bloated, yellow-green, like something fleshy that had been discolored by long submersion.

"Joe," Father said in a strained, monotone voice, "I got to ask you to let me see that drum."

"Why, sure—" Joe's voice seemed strained, too; in the glisteny, pallid blubber of his features his lips were swollen violet, wobbling as if they might come off. "What'sa matter, Sheriff? I hit a bump back there, an' thought I heard th' heads crack. Wet weather plays hob with drumheads. Yeah—I stopped to loosen her up—"

He pushed the drum forward as Father unlimbered from the car. Stood there round-shouldered, saggy, his stary eyes on my father's face. Father's eyes looked even queerer as he hefted the drum, hit it a thump with clenched knuckles, shoved it back to Joe, then went to the bridge-rail and stared out into the mist-swirl.

"Joe," turning carelessly, "my kid here wants me to buy him

one of those bass drums when he gets to high school. What they cost?"

"Wha—what they cost?" The big man's face altered like squeezed dough. Became familiar. "Why—why, anywhere fifty to a hundred bucks, Sheriff. One like mine."

"What's one of those foot-pedals they use in these city dance bands cost, Joe?"

"Two-fifty mail order if—" he broke off, coughing; pulled his palm across his lips. "I dunno, Sheriff. Never used one. Well, I better get that drum outa th' wet before it—"

"Joe," Father interrupted, "why'd you buy three balls of twine at Clapp's store a few days ago?"

"Say—!" the voice slid plaintively off key. "What is this—?"

"Well, only this, Joe. Suppose a person, if any, was comin' down th' path goes by your summerhouse. Summerhouse, there, is about three hundred feet from th' big house. Clapp says those balls of twine he sells are about a hundred feet long. Three balls, three hundred feet, say. Maybe a little extra left over. Enough to make a noose—"

Joe's mouth gaped. "A noose—?"

Father nodded. "Big enough to hang a person."

A thread of saliva glistened down Joe's chin, like the trail left by a snail. "Hang a—say, you don't think—! You don't think my wife—murdered by—somebody threw a noose around her neck an'—"

"Noose was around your own neck, I'd say, Joe. Around your wrist, really. Let's say th' cord was hiked up over th' limb of a locust tree by th' summerhouse, and the other end went back into your bedroom window and was tied to one of those foot-pedals attached to your drum. Let's say you kept it beating for two reasons—alibi to make th' village and your wife think you were all the time in the house—and somethin' to cover th' sound of a shot. Let's say th' sound was muffled, too, by a burlap bag—the one you used afterwards to carry th' body in. You meant to get rid of it that night, let's say, but you didn't dare go out after midnight on account of it rained and your tracks might 've showed in th' mud. You'd stowed this body under ice in your woodshed, and you have to leave it there a while. Knowin' your wife's absence in the village would start plenty of talk, you figured you'd start it yourself to avoid suspicion. That's why you came to me about it. But you didn't figure on me finding th' forty-five shell. Then you had to think fast, so you figured you'd better make it look like Spiritualistic hokus-pokus, an' last night you cut those capers around town, killin' your cat and chucking it under Floss Watters' window, then playin' ghost under a sheet. Norman played right into your hands, an' so did the others. But you still had that body in the ice—"

Breath that had been gathering in Joe's lungs squalled out, "I never killed her!"

"—you still had that body in the ice," Father's words went on in that unswerving monotone, "and you had to get it outa that shed. So you hit on the idea of bringin' it with you over to Brockton. You pulled that stunt with your wife's picture—I saw where it'd been moved off th' wall and maybe taken outa th' frame—holdin' it behind th' curtains when Mrs. Sailor went by the house, to scare her. You did that to draw th' whole town to your house, thinkin' you could drive on to Brockton by yourself. You wanted a chance to heave th' body in th' river on your way across th' bridge—delaying so it'd be dark time you got there. Only I followed you over; you didn't get the chance; and then you had to lug that body around in the only place you could carry it without it being seen until—"

THE BIG MAN'S face was again out of shape; his eyes like a cat's, green exclamation points blazing in yellow zeros. "You're crazy! Crazy's hell! I tell you, Sheriff, I never killed her! It's those damn village gossips sayin' I wanted of get rid of my wife so's I could claim her property an' hike off afterward with Myrtle. I never killed Carrie Sleeper, Sheriff. I swear I never—"

"No, you didn't kill your wife, Joe, that's right. Here's a wire from Albany about her."

He handed the telegram to Joe; watched horror grow on the big drummer's features as he held the paper under the car-lights. But once since that time have I seen an expression anything like it. During the War when an artillery officer discovered that by miscalculation he'd been pouring shells into our own men. But that face was nothing to Joe Sleeper's. A single red vein ran from temple to temple like a miniature zigzag of lightning under the flesh. The eyeballs, as if electrocuted, bulged. Cheeks sloughed down into jowls; mouth ruptured open.

It was a strange sound the fellow made then. Like an "Awk!" of a chicken at ax-fall.

He was over the bridge-rail as he made it, vaulting drum and railing in one leap. Paused for an instant in blowing mist, arms widespread, legs kicking, a shadow on a cloud, there and gone. It seemed I could have counted ten before the splash. Black waters showered high, and Father sprang back at our car, shouting for the lantern in the back seat.

They found Joe's body down by Appleby's ice house next morning, drowned and the neck broken. Right under the bridge they found one of those foot-pedals dance bands use for drums, a length of brown twine knotted to the hinge where Joe had cut it off in a hurry. And in the deep part under the bridge, weighted with rocks and its burden, they found the burlap sack. I was sorry I was there to see its contents. When I thought of how I'd carried the drum at the Brockton Fair, how heavy it was (even with Joe lugging more than his share), how cold it seemed, and how the body in the bag, frozen stiff from two days on ice, thawing, must have struck the drumhead with a relaxing elbow. But I don't think about that much.

Also in the bag they found an old Spanish War .45. The gun with which Joe Sleeper, hiding in the black rendezvous of the summerhouse, waiting his wife's return from that prearranged visit to Blackberry Hill, and seeing a woman's shadow on the path in the moonless dark, had shot Myrtle Dockstader—killed his accomplice as she hurried to bring him wonderful news—

slew his love in the dark with a bullet squarely between her eyes.

No, I didn't want a bass drum when I got to high school, and I don't want one now. I know better instruments. Piccolos.

V

DAISIES WON'T TELL

*A wolf came to Four Corners in
black sheep's clothing.*

PEOPLE WHO SAW him that afternoon thought he was an old, old man. Like a shadow he drifted into Four Corners, thin and doddery and white-headed as an autumn dandelion brought there on the dusty wind. Nondescript in shabby clothes, he would have passed unnoticed through the village but for the bloodless pallor of his face, the blue-veined whiteness of ancient hands, and the strange watery brilliance of eager eyes.

A queer excitement seemed to overcome him when he stopped to buy a shovel in the general store; his hands shook so violently he dropped his change. Poor as Poverty he looked, yet he gave a queer hollow laugh at the accident, and told the startled storekeeper to keep the money.

Then at the corner near First Church he stopped to rest against a tree, and seemed bewildered of his way, staring about him in a manner confused. Mule Lickette went by, and he quavered at Mule a question about the road to Butternut Hill. Mule pointed it out obligingly, and the old, old man started off with a briskness that astonished the villager. And there was something eerie about him, something almost scary to Mule. The last Mule saw of him was the metallic flash of the shovel as the old man topped the ridge above Blue Valley and took the brown country road eastward toward the vine-grown ruins of the old Curlew house.

ANY FAMILY is liable to have a skeleton in the closet—leastwise, any doctor's family. Sometimes there's more than one.

Generally the phrase implies a subject that isn't discussed beyond the Thanksgiving dinner table; usually something scandalous, like Cousin Harry's marriage to a burlesque dancer, or something mysterious, like Aunt Joe being seen in New Orleans when her letters were coming from Chicago, or something shameful, like Doc Curlew's grandson robbing the village tavern when he was sixteen and then running away to Australia after Doc had paid plenty to hush it up.

They said it broke the old doctor's heart. "It isn't that Andy is a bad boy," he'd apologized when the kid was in previous scrapes (like the time he put a shotgun shell in the schoolhouse stove, and the teacher'd almost lost a finger building the fire.) "It's just that he never had any parents but Gramma and me. Reckon I've gave him more money than was good for him, and Gramma indulged him too much. But I'm going to make a doctor out of him. You'll see. Give him another chance. He's a good boy."

But after he'd robbed the tavern, the old doctor was through. "Don't ever mention that scoundrel's name in this house again!" he thundered at Gramma. "He's dead as far as this family is concerned. Understand? Dead!" When a letter came from Australia whining for money to get home, the old doctor tore it up. He tore up three more letters without Gramma knowing about them or answering them. After that there was no more word of the boy. They said the old doctor died of heart-break.

Gramma put away the doctor's medical things and closed up his room and lived alone in the big wide house overlooking the big wide farm above Blue Valley. That was in 1891.

In 1903 the following notice appeared in the "personals" column of a New York newspaper.

> Will Andrew Curlew, or anyone having information concerning the whereabouts of Andrew Curlew—black hair, brown eyes, height about five feet seven, scar on back left hand, age twenty-seven—last heard from, Brisbane, Australia, twelve years ago—please communicate with Mrs. Nathaniel Curlew, R.F.D. 7, Four Corners? His grandmother is lonely and wants him back.

THE FRONT room over Cleggy's Bowery Bar was dim and hot, and the sullen, hard-faced man, whose eyeballs were points of furious light gleaming through red-edged cracks, paced the floor like a cooped-up animal. Noises of the Bowery, the rattle of drays, trolley-clang, boom and shock of a passing elevated train, shook through the drawn window-blinds on gusts of July heat. Outside was life and freedom. Freedom! He couldn't even go down to the barroom below and cool his throat on a beer. Jails were better than this. And there it was again. That tin piano! If he had to listen to that blasted ditty again he'd go crazy.

He listened to it, fists clenched, eyes glaring at the floor.

Daisy, Daisy, give me your answer, do—

All day. All night. They must've played the blasted tune at least ten thousand times since he'd been nailed up in this lousy hide-out. He glared at the vibrating floor. Laughter down there. Women. Some hoarse men's voices picking up the chorus as they thumped on tables with beer mugs. "I'm most cray-zy, over thah love uh yoooo." Blast them, couldn't they play something else beside that stale piece? Why didn't they play *Two Little Girls In Blue* or *Pony Boy* or *Yip I Yaddy I Yay?* That constant repetition was enough to drive a guy off his nut. And he hated that *Bicycle Built For Two* song. The words, "Daisy, Daisy" got on his nerves.

Music always brings memories, becomes associated with certain incidents, episodes, places. For the hard-faced man that tune had unpleasant associations. Took him back to a jailhouse on the Barbary Coast; four lantern-jawed cops standing over him with nightsticks. Across the street in a saloon they were whooping that song. The cops were trying to get him to talk, and he wouldn't open his mouth. They'd ask a question, then slap him on the muscle with a nightstick when he wouldn't answer. Then throw water on him to bring him around. "You're a daisy, you are," one of the cops had said at the last, just before crashing the club down on his head. The name had stuck.

It was a dangerous nickname to own, right now. Plastered all over the papers and post offices. Made his teeth feel furry to hear them bellering it in song in the barroom downstairs. If he ever got his hands on the guy who wrote that ditty, he could kill him. Yeah, kill—

"Huh!" A knock on the door caught him in the middle of his thought, and the man pulled a breath and jerked his hands behind him as if to conceal what had passed through his mind. Under the floor the tin piano was starting it again. Tensely, the hard-faced man glared at the door. The knock was repeated. Three taps, then two. He muttered, "Goggles." Relaxed cords loosened the set of his jaw; slipping key from pocket, he sidled to the door, opened a careful inch, then jerked it wide.

Blare of music and a plump ripe-nosed man with ten gold teeth and protruberant hazel eyes entered the room swiftly. The hard-faced man slapped the door shut furtively; put his back against it as if to keep the music out. His eyes angered at the plump man who was depositing a brown derby and a portfolio on the littered table.

He took a step forward.

"Well, what do *you* want?"

The plump man turned around, smiling. "I want a steak at Delmonico's, the third girl from the right at Rector's, and a go at Canfield's."

"How would you like a bash in the mouth?"

The plump man nodded merrily. "You're th' boy as could give it to me, Daisy, me lad. Yes, sir, no doubt about that. No doubt at all."

A savage oath filed through the other's teeth. Brows drawn, he walked at his visitor menacingly. "Listen, Goggles, you get me out of this dump, or that mouth of yours will think it was hit by the California gold rush. Twenty days! Twenty days I been tied up in this garret, not even darin' to put up th' winda shades. Nothin' decent to eat. Nothin' to do but sit here thinkin' any minute a flatfoot may walk in. Listenin' all the time to that damn *Bicycle Built For Two* ditty downstairs. I'll go batty if I don't get outa here! I can't stand bein' shut up! I can't stand it!" Elbows cocked at his sides, he advanced slowly on the fat man; his hands a little in front of him, fingers pointed, thumbs up like triggers, curiously like a lobster's nippers. He whispered, "I'd rather hang for croaking those two dames in Frisco than sit in this room another hour. I oughta wring yer neck, Goggles! You got me inta this jam, an' by Judas! you'll get me out, or—"

"Daisy," the plump man murmured, retreating a step, "you've got the nicest black hair."

The hard face cemented in an astonished glare.

"And the nicest brown eyes."

"Say what the—!"

"And just the right height—five feet seven in your—"

INCREDULITY, wrestling with fury on the hard man's features, had lost. His fingers whipped out; caught his visitor by the necktie. "What's the joke, Goggles?" he panted. "Why the one-two-three skiddoo? If you've come up here to kid me, I'll pull the tonsils outa your throat the way I'd core an apple. I'll—"

"The scar," gurgled the fat man imperturbably, "would be easy. Take off some skin with a razor, and some lye to turn it blue."

"I'll turn *you* blue, you pop-eyed shyster, if you don't tell—"

"Daisy Boy—Daisy Boy—" the plump man strangled reproachfully. "You wouldn't blink—a pal—?"

"Wouldn't I? Didn't I tell you never to call me by that moniker again?"

Laughter bubbling from the fat man's throttled neck was so astonishing that the nippers let go. Gasping, the fat man backed away, feeling his collar, eyes full of tears but merry. "Whew—! You still got your grip, Daisy Boy. Wait—!" hastily. "That's the last time you'll ever hear that name, so help me. From now on it's Andy. Get used to it. *Andy.*"

Downstairs the tin piano was plunking. "Daisy, Daisy—" In the dim splutter of the gaslight, the hard man's features were yellowish, baffled. His mouth twisted down at one corner. He twisted out, "I don't get the drift of this. You got somethin' up your sleeve, Goggles. What?"

"A couple of hundred thousand dollars."

"A couple of hundred thousand whaaat—?"

"Dollars," the fat man beamed. "So easy it's like takin' 'em outa your own pocket," the fat man twinkled. "I was up to this place over the week-end just to scout around, and I found out all about it." The fat man's face was rosy as a Billikin's. "Some of it's in cash, some of it's in property, an' half of it's in diamonds." A golden grin spread wide across the fat man's features and seemed to light up the room.

"Goggles," the whisper came like a knife, "if this's a joke—"

The grin became a blaze. "I'm telling you, her husband was a rich sawbones and left her these heirlooms when he died. Three sparklers big as New York. She keeps 'em right in the house, if you can imagine it, and there's this farm, besides. Pal, I know the whole family history from A to Z, and I didn't even have to ask about the kid. It's the kind of one-horse burg where they leave the doors open at night. He got the scar from a horse stamping on his hand when he was five. Broke his ankle stealing melons when he was ten. Swiped some money when he was sixteen, and the old sawbones kicked him out. Nobody's seen or heard of him for twelve years. The old lady's half blind to make it easier, and he'd be a changed man, anyhow, bumming around Australia all this time. Pal," the fat man puffed down in a chair and smiled delight at the hard-faced one, "it's a cinch!"

An elevated train shook sooty heat through the window shades, and the hard man's hands were lobster nippers, again "For two cents," he told his visitor, "I'd pinch that head of blubber off your neck!"

The fat man clucked as if he'd just hatched an egg. "For two hundred thousand you don't even have to kill anybody; all you gotta do is wait for this old dame to die. Ever hear of a place called Four Corners? You're going to. Boy," said the fat man in a high, twittering voice, "I'm right glad to see you home again. You've changed some since you been in Australia, Andy boy, but you still got the same black hair an' nice brown eyes. Let me be the first to welcome you, Andy old grandson. I always did want to go halvers with a guy who stood to inherit two hundred thousand dollars."

Opening his portfolio, the plump one handed his stunned listener a notice. A clipping from the "personals" column of a New York paper. Then the only sound in the room was the song under the floor, until the fat man chuckled, "The kid's dead, see? I defended him in a murder trial ten years ago in Brisbane, and I was the only one there who knew his right name."

It was evident from the hard man's eyes that he saw.

GRAMMA CURLEW was puzzled and disturbed. Not by the change in Andy, for a stripling becomes a man in twelve years and all sorts of alterations may develop in his make-up, and, too, her specs were apt to blur people's faces out of focus. It wasn't his reluctance to talk or the way he avoided folks, either— natural that he'd be kind of shy and silent, coming back like this. No, it was something she couldn't put a finger on; something alien about him that didn't seem kin. He was Andy grown up, that was all, and yet there was something furtive or foreign or unnatural about him, she couldn't tell what.

Wasn't like a Curlew to be forgetful, for one thing. The Curlews all had wonderful memories. Yet when she'd told him to take his luggage right up to his old room, he'd halted on the stairway, blankly; said he'd been away so long he didn't remember where it was. And the barn. He'd forgotten the name of his pet rooster, and mistaken barley for oats and straw for hay. He didn't recognize Aunt Kat in the family album, or recall Cousin Ambrose's being killed at Cold Harbour. And only today when she'd come in from the greenhouse with a basket of daisies on her arm—a rare variety of black-eyed susans she'd imported from the South intending to transplant them in a window box—he'd called them flowers, and asked what kind they were. She'd put the basket on the kitchen table to stare at him. For years she had cultivated those plants in her greenhouse; they'd been the doctor's favorite blossom and were the only ones of their kind in Blue Valley. "Why, Andy, don't you remember? I had to spank you once for picking them. Those are black-eyed susans! *Daisies!*" He'd looked so queer when she spoke the name. She recalled, now, that in her surprise she'd left them there in the kitchen. He'd seemed upset; and she'd followed him out to the porch.

Sometimes it didn't seem like Andy at all. Something in his eyes? More likely in her own eyes; these stupid spectacles. Likely the boy'd had a pretty hard time of it, at the end of the world in that God-forsaken country. Enough to age any man. Funny about that forgetfulness, though. He could remember very well about the horse stepping on his hand and giving him that scar—that was when he was five. He couldn't remember black-eyed susans, daisies he'd seen in the greenhouse all his boyhood days.

"I expect you may find me kinda strange," he'd told her on the day of his return. "It's just that I been away twelve years."

Of course. The letter from that lawyer who'd found him in New York had warned her about that:

> *Your grandson seems to have been through a great deal, and he was somewhat anxious about you recognising him. He is naturally reluctant about discussing his past, and feels he already owes you more than he could ever repay. I have urged him to return, however, and showed him your last letter, at which he burst into tears of repentance and gratitude. So I have finally prevailed upon him to accept your offer of railroad fare and—*

How nice that lawyer had been, returning her fee and saying he was glad to be God's instrument in this happy reunion. Gramma sighed. What *was* the matter with her tonight? It was good to have the boy back. Yes, and every minute he'd been back, he'd been so thoughtful of her. Always helping her to her room at night. Coming in to tuck in a blanket. Running to fetch her slippers, her smelling salts, her Bible. It was just the moustache that made his face seem different. These specs. She'd have to get another pair. Only—

She smiled at memory of a little boy, wistfully. Then scolded herself for having worried. Andy was back, that was all that mattered.

Folding the Bible, she put it on the bedside table. God had been kind. She adjusted her nightcap, turned down the kerosene lamp and rested back on the pillows, with a good-night look at the doctor's picture on the bureau. "You wanted Andy back, didn't you?" she nodded at the picture. Long shadows walked up the wall beyond the foot of her bed, bedpost shadows that were friends of hers in the big empty room. Albert the cat snored soundlessly on the patchwork quilt, and a night-bird chirped in the sleepy elm that stood guard by the open window. All friends of Gramma's. But Andy was home, now, and they didn't need to worry. And she'd been glad to be able to send the hired man and his wife to the tenant cottage down the road. The house belonged to the Curlews again.

Only she wished Andy felt more comfortable in it. Not so

shy about Four Corners. Couldn't blame him for coming on a night train like he had, and hurrying through the village without stopping to say hello, but he'd ought to begin seeing his old friends again. They'd think it was queer. For the three weeks since he'd been here, he'd hardly stepped outside the gate. Unhealthy for a boy to keep to his room like he was.

Gramma pushed up her spectacles; listened. He was in his room now. Awake. Pacing. Like he had every night since he'd come back. She could hear the measured foot-treads—*pace, pace, pace*—one thing Gramma had was ears. My! and it was most one o'clock. An old woman didn't need any sleep, but a man ought to get a-plenty. But she hadn't spoken to him about it, wanting him to have his own way, get used to things, the feeling of being home. Men were like dogs, it took 'em a while to settle down. Andy'd been on ships where you walked up and down half the night on watch. Habit.

The scamp. She rather wished he'd tell a little about his adventures; they'd be interesting. Now that she and the doctor had forgiven his boyish escapades, he'd ought to forgive himself. Ever since he'd been back, he'd done nothing but apologize, and being sorry wasn't healthy. She'd have to put a stop to that. He mustn't feel like a prodigal or anything.

Pace, pace, pace—

Could it be the boy's conscience was bothering him? Every growing boy gets into scrapes. Maybe if she could say something to put him at his ease—invite over a couple of girls who hadn't been in town when—

Pace, pace, pace—

Gramma's head lifted from the pillows. Why—why, Andy had left his room. Was he sick? Those footsteps were coming up the hall. Toward her door. They—

Click! He was turning the knob. Coming in to see her. He—

Instinct is a curious thing. Glasses on forehead, the old lady saw him only as a blur, yet something about the way he opened her bedroom door and stood there, filled her with cold alarm.

Albert the cat woke instantly and went *pfffft!* Andy was holding a candle, and his shadow in the hall behind him was long and black and stealthy. He placed the candle on the bureau and moved slowly toward the bed, taller, taller, taller. In a thrall of tension the old lady's vision cleared; she saw his face stark and rigid, the wolfish set of his jaws, the merciless teeth, the eyes that were savage green balls. Gramma sat bolt upright in terror.

Elbows cocked, he advanced slowly, his hands a little in front of him, fingers pointed, thumbs up like triggers, curiously like a lobster's nippers.

"The diamonds!" he was whispering. "It's no use hollering, old woman, there ain't a soul within a mile of the house. I want them diamonds—!"

HE HAD to grin at the expression on her face. The old woman was paralyzed. Bet she was sorry now she'd took his advice and sent that hired man and his wife to the cottage away down the road. Might let out a squawk any minute, but he could stop that quick enough, and the nearest neighbor was half a mile. And if she wouldn't talk? Well, he'd make her. Not many men could keep their lips buttoned the way *he* could, and this was an old woman. Couple of minutes with that candle against the soles of her feet, and he'd be in Canada with those diamonds in his pocket, one-two-three skiddoo.

Everything was jake. Three-Eyed Mike was ready with horse and buggy at that border town, and Steve the peterman would put him up in Montreal. All he wished was he could see Goggle's fat face when he learned about it. This was one time that shyster couldn't squeal.

That fat snail! Taking none of the risk, and wanting fifty-fifty. Just for cooking up the swindle and writing a few letters. Sat back on his cushion in New York while he, Daisy Boy Dumont, chanced his neck in this old woman's house where any second some rube might step in and spike the game. No matter how much he'd rehearsed, sooner or later he was bound to slip, and already there'd been a bunch of close calls. He

couldn't sit in his room much longer without it looking suspicious—confinement always got on his nerves—and this farm
life would drive him batty. Besides, the old dame might live
another ten years. Goggles said she was sure to leave him the
property, but the risk was too long. It was typical of Daisy Boy
Dumont that he planned the double-cross on the night when
Goggles first proposed the scheme.

Teeth bared, he leaned over the frail figure petrified in the
bed. "You may as well tell me where the stones are hid," he
advised Gramma in a low guttural. "I been all over th' house
since I come here, but there's doors I couldn't open, and I got
no time to jimmy the whole place. We're alone in th' house,
Granny. If you don't hand over th' sparklers, I'll croak you!"

He had no intention of adding another death-sentence to
his record; these Eastern police were too tough. But his threat
had to be convincing. If he didn't get those gems tonight, he'd
never get them. And the house was too big to frisk all the rooms.
He'd have to make her talk.

"Andy," she whispered. "Andy Curlew—"

"Did you hear me say I'd croak you?"

"Your own grandmother!"

"Grandmother be blowed! Where are they?" Wheeling, he
snatched the candle from the bureau; moved at her in a stoop.

She saw the look in his eyes, and she understood the candle.
Gramma could remember the Indians. But she was an old
woman, and she knew she would be unable to stand the phys-
ical torture.

"You're going to burn my feet," she whispered. "You're going
to torture a helpless old woman—"

"I want those diamond rings!"

He thought the trembling wrinkles about her mouth meant
fear. He didn't see the light that kindled suddenly in her faded
eyes. "Criminal!" Bolt upright under the covers, she confronted
him with an unexpected fierceness that drove him back a step,
her eyes blazing under the fringe of her nightcap, a tiny, electri-

fied figure in that vast and shadowy bed, her voice quivering in a high, eerie triumph that flustered the man.

"Criminal!" she quavered fiercely. "I knew you could not be Andy Curlew! Whatever that boy did, he meant no evil! You are wicked, cruel, unclean! I'm glad! I can see you now as I could not see you with my eyes! Andy is dead and you are somebody else! An impostor! A lie! You are not my grandson!" Shadows grew up the wall behind her as she pointed in triumphant accusation. "God will punish you for this crime; do you hear? God will punish you! He will blight your days, and from now till you die, you will go as one accursed!"

He leaned at her, panting. "Why, you crazy old witch—!"

"Wait!" she cried at him, "I know! You will torture me for the diamonds! Greed does not stand long in fear of God! You would torture me and find them! But they were meant for Andy, meant for my grandson, not for you! God is going to punish you—*now*—!"

Stunned by that strange outcry, he sprang too late. He saw her hand go under her lace collar; saw the flash of the rings on the pink ribbon she tore from her throat. White fire shimmered in the candle beams; vanished as she clapped her hand to her mouth. Daisy Boy Dumont yelled. The cat squalled underfoot, tripping him, and his outflung fingers dropped the candle. Gramma's laugh choked off, *wheeee!* in his face, and for a dreadful instant her open mouth seemed to sparkle.

Too late he caught her throat, squeezing, trying to block the passage. Seeing his face in that final moment of her consciousness, Gramma knew she had won. He heard a spasm of strangly laughter, a sound like *glou, glou, glou*. He howled, "Give them up! Give them up!" shaking her, pounding her back in a desperate effort to dislodge the obstruction. Sweat burst on his forehead as he saw her discolored lips, suffocating eyes. Black shadows danced and writhed and twisted on the wall above the bed as Gramma's throat gave a last gulping convulsion. Then Gramma and the diamonds were gone.

The man's eyes were butterplates of horror and unbelief. "She's swallowed them!"

HANDS limp, shaking, his face the more distorted of the two, Daisy Boy Dumont backed away from the death bed. Cheated, that's what he was! Ninety thousand dollars' worth of Tiffany's cheated right out from his grasp. And that wasn't all. Through the red haze of rage and bafflement, he was suddenly aware of the old lady's glassy and sightless eyes, the big silent house around him, the soundlessness of rural night. Fear. It enveloped him like an icy wind; left him staring, rigid. That body on the bed. The hired man coming with the morning. Coroner's investigation. Autopsy. How'd those diamonds get there?

He shouted at the big, shadowed room, "She committed suicide! Swallowed those rings and choked herself to death!"

And the cops would never believe it. Never! They'd be hounding him for a murder he didn't commit. The thought held him addled in terror and he blurted, "Geez!" his swivelling eyes panic-stricken. He'd have to get out of here, beat it, hide! But where? Goggles would know he'd tried to double-cross him. No money to smuggle himself into Canada. This crazy old witch had trapped him, killed herself to bring the cops down on him.

In his panic he could almost hear the baying of imaginary hounds, and he fled to the bedroom window and had one leg over the sill, body braced to jump, when he glimpsed another way out. With an oath, he pulled himself back from the frame. Stared. At landscape black and green and silver in cloudy moonlight. At the far night-misted sweep of Blue Valley, the down-rolling meadowland of the Curlew farm, slopes laced with winding cow streams and grassy pastures asleep in summer dark. Only the corner of his eye was aware of this nocturnal panorama; his stare had fixed on the big dark barn in the foreground, the moon-shadowed barnyard, a shovel leaning there against the barn door. A shovel! As if through a burst of lightning, Daisy Boy Dumont saw it all. Even to the doctor he knew about in Canada, the crooked surgeon he'd write to come jumping and bring his tools. Even to the story he'd tell these Four Corners hicks about the old lady going to New York.

"Pull a trick on me, will she? I'll have those jools yet!"

Turning about from the window, he had to laugh. Why, it was even better this way—if he'd beat it with the gems and left the old woman roped to the bed as he'd planned, he'd have had the cops to deal with anyhow. Leaping at the bed, he scooped up the fragile, still figure in its blankets, and scuttled out into the hall. By the time he reached the stairs his wits were in running order again. It would not be the first time Daisy Boy Dumont had jumped a trap.

Then the daisies in the kitchen were pure inspiration. He saw the basket on the table where Gramma had left them that morning, the uprooted flowers she'd been transplanting in her garden. Broad fields might become puzzling in day time, and he'd need a marker that wouldn't look suspicious.

Nobody saw him take the cow-path for the lower meadows, and if anyone had, he was only a farmer out to dig a bear-pit with a sack of bait on his shoulder and an armful of weeds to mask the snare. Owls and the smell of damp fields—he liked the night. Keeping to a shallow gulley, he made for a cloudy thicket of aspen, but the rooted earth proved too difficult for digging, and his instinct advised a further retreat from the house.

For a man waterfront bred, he chose his location well—beyond view of the house and highroad, on the far side of rolling open slope in a clover meadow wide as the sky. In case of suspicion they'd scout the valley woods; no one would think to search open pasture land somewhere in the middle of the farm. He waited a moment, spitting on his hands, while the moon put her face behind a cloud.

THE LOAM made easy spading. Daisy Boy worked with an industry beaverish and single-minded, intent on his task, enjoying the sweat of his brow and the ripening fruits of his labor. Three feet was deep enough, and filling the grave was even easier. It was done. He finished the mound with an artistic shovel pat and an obscene, "See you next week, Grandma!" and—by Cripes!—it was just like putting money in the bank. Grinning, he dropped dog-fashion to his knees and set to work replacing the turf and planting daisies.

But he was not to see Gramma next week or a good many weeks after that; he had just finished planting the last daisy when he had his first hint of disaster—noticed for the first time the singe in the air and the tinge of crimson on his hands.

"What the devil—!"

Daisy Boy Dumont spun in fear. Above the slope where he stood revealed, the sky was a band of light. Crimson brightened to scarlet as he stared, chasing back the edges of the night, flooding hill crest and pasture as with a dye of blood. The light stretched and grew like some infernal sunrise. Somewhere a rooster crowed.

Appalled, the man clutched his shovel and ran. He was aware of a smarting pungence, a thickening sulphurous haze; a noise like far-off shouting that loudened to a drumming roar as he raced up the cowpath. Now he could distinguish a sound like the popping of corks; under the deeper undertone a crackling of splintering sticks, small explosions, a vast rustling as of wind in corn. A baleful pall of yellow smoke coiled sluggishly against the tinted sky. All the trees on the hill crest were leafed in gold.

His breath choked as he ran.

He rounded the barn at the moment the house roof burst into vivid incandescence. In the village across Blue Valley the fire whistle shrieked. Flinging aside the shovel, Daisy Boy Dumont rushed in panic for the gate, only to see the dust of oncoming wagons, the weaving line of rigs, galloping teams, horses, dogs, bicycles speeding up the awakened country road. From ridge to ridge the valley was out of its bed. Farmers were running cross-lots in the reddened meadows; men yelled in the pasture below him; and as Daisy Boy Dumont wheeled and gasped in a terror of indecision, a horseman charged through the smoke-hidden gate and rode down on him, shouting.

"Where's Gramma Curlew? Where's Gramma Curlew?"

He saw the sheriff's star before he could run, and his voice was a squeal above the holocaustal thunder. "She ain't in the house—there ain't nobody in the house—She's in New York—!"

And the next thing he knew, he was under arrest for murder.

What Daisy Boy Dumont did not know that night, and one of the things he would never know, was that Gramma's last kick had sent her Bible within reach of the fallen candle.

TO THIS DAY Four Corners talks about the trial, painting the scene with the vivid colors of recollection only a little more lurid for the mixture of hard cider and imagination—brushing up the high-lights—adding the touch of caricature—dusting off for local memory the tense, packed hush of County Court House; the awesome jowls of old Judge Lamb; the thundering and posturing of lawyers drunk on old-school eloquence: solemn witnesses taking oaths; the jury of faces like tintypes; the windows festooned with small boys; the audience applauding each new disclosure with a general indrawing of breath; all eyes focussed on the accused—

In the memory of Four Corners, he sat there "like a man already dead." Lockjawed. Staring. His face the color of the ashes blowing in the Curlew barnyard.

And well he might, for Aminidab Coward, the Little Giant, was Prosecution, and the malefactor who escaped that nemesis of oratory, accusations, and cunning legal traps, was a lucky and unknown man. Coward had his fierce blue eyes on the state capital that year, and his integrity and ability were no whit lessened by his ambition. In his left hand he carried high the torch as Public Avenger; in his right, the Hammer of Justice with which, blow by deadly blow, he would nail shut his case. Trials were dramatic with Coward holding the floor. Defense, accused and audience could always be tensely certain he would seal the lid with some stunning surprise.

"You have had bared for you," he summed up to the jury, "the character of Andrew Curlew. You have heard John Sailor, owner of our local tavern, describe the well-known episode of the robbery. Mr. Dillinghill, our respected schoolmaster, has disclosed the defendant's unruly conduct as a pupil in his classroom. Witness after witness has testified as to the early life of the accused, his ingratitude toward his benefactors, his wild youth, his bad reputation which broke his poor grandfather's heart. Has the accused denied these facts? How could he? Has my illustrious colleague of the Defense disproved these evidences of the corrupt character of his client as a youth? No! Both learned counsel and accused have uttered no reply to these statements save to object to their pertinency to the homicide case.

"Gentlemen of the jury, the boy is father to the man. I give you a youthful robber, ingrate and vagabond. I give you that character sinking to the depths of murder. The learned counsel of the Defense has asked what motive. What motive, gentlemen of the jury? You saw the face of the accused when poor Grandmother Curlew's attorney disclosed how she had left this grandson everything in her will. He says he did not know of her will. Yet only a week before the fire she visited her attorney and changed her will so that this grandson might inherit the lands and money of the Curlew estate and the famous Curlew diamonds. Is it possible the accused urged her to do so? Is it possible—but we are not dealing with possibilities. The law must decide by established facts.

"Gentlemen of the jury, you have heard the members of our brave fire department declare the fire to have been of incendiary origin in their opinion. You have heard the testimony as to the peculiar quality of the smoke and the hint of chemicals. Learned counsel of the Defense has tried to wave aside the fact of the quick-spread conflagration by pointing to the dryness of the previous weather and the lack of fire-fighting equipment. However, all that is beside my point. Gentlemen of the jury, Sheriff Whittier has testified that when he reached the scene of the fire, he discovered the defendant at the gate, and asked him the whereabouts of Grandmother Curlew. You have heard the defendant's answer: she was in New York. We will not bother to examine his strange story of her sudden departure to the great metropolis, called thither by a telegram from an unknown solicitor—we will not dwell on the fact that our local telegraph operator can find no record of such a message, or the fact that the conductor of the train cannot remember Grandmother Curlew among his passengers. Nor will we dwell on the fact that, although hunted by the efficient police of that great city, she has not yet been found in New York, although six months since the fire have gone by. We will dwell only on the defendant's declaration that there was nobody in the burning house. Remember his words. *There was nobody in the burning house!*"

Wherewith Aminidab Coward turned his smoldering blue eyes on Judge Lamb and asked to introduce a final and extraordinary bit of evidence. Then, would Sheriff Dan Whittier please take the stand? Would Sheriff Dan Whittier kindly tell the jury what he had found among the charred ruins of the noble old mansion on Butternut Hill during the week following the fire?

"Well, the place was pretty well burnt down, but th' fire company had saved some of th' downstairs. I thought I'd kind of poke around, havin' already arrested Andrew Curlew for arson, and wanting some more definite evidence than th' chemical smell to the smoke. Everything was ashes and black timbers, but there was this closet in a back room and the door, although burnt to a crisp, was still standing, and it was locked. Fire Chief Ganning was with me, and we busted in. The inside of th' closet was gutted by the fire, but—but we found something."

"With the permission of the Court I will ask you to show the jury what was there in that locked and fire-consumed closet."

It was like Aminidab Coward. The dramatic suitcase placed on the stand. The breathless pause, then the tantalizing declaration that the contents of this suitcase were all that had remained of what had been in that locked closet in the burning Curlew house. The slow unlatching of the suitcase. The bones

ranged one by one on the table before the horrified stares of
judge, jury and courtroom; the horrified stare of the accused.

Not many bones. Aminidab Coward described them as he
lined them up in that grim array. A femur. A knuckle. The
clavicle. A human rib.

"Out of that furnace they come as sole evidence of a das-
tardly pyre," swore Aminidab Coward, pointing. "And lastly, as
proof of homicide—"

A fire-blackened skull. The lower jaw burned away; the
charred eyeholes staring a hollow and awful accusation at the
ghastly eyes of the accused.

Aminidab Coward exploded the question as a bombshell.
"Before God, Andrew Curlew, I am asking you! *Who was in
that locked closet?*"

THIRTY years! Thirty years condemned to the living death
of a lifetime sentence for a murder he had not committed! He
had been framed. Framed by that damned district attorney who
had his eyes on the state capital. And to his screaming appeals
and denials they had only put the one deadly question: *Then
where is Grandmother Curlew?*

What could he say? Every door to escape had closed on him
in a succession of steel-sprung traps. To deny he was Andrew
Curlew meant identification as Daisy Boy Dumont, wanted
for two other murders—and ones he *had* committed—on the
Barbary Coast. To declare the true whereabouts of Grandmother Curlew meant—Oh, how they had framed him!

Still, he had not cracked. Before all the lightning and thunder
of that cursed prosecutor, he had kept his jaw locked about
those diamonds. Searchers had combed the ruins for them; the
law had badgered him with every device to wring from him a
confession concerning those vanished gems, and he had shut
his teeth against speech in a day when the Third Degree was
the Third Degree.

But thirty years! His defense counsel had had the nerve to
tell him he was lucky. Only doubt concerning the identity of

those bones had saved him from the death cell. But thirty years to a man who hated confinement was a living death-cell, every day and hour poisoned by the injustice of false condemnation. And Goggles, there at the gate to grin at him as he went in. The fat swine giving him a wink as the irons clanged. Daisy Boy Dumont would have died that first day behind bars but for the incident that had saved him from self destruction.

As they marched him to the Warden's Office for his shave and haircut and number, their route passed a flower garden. Trusties were grubbing among the plants, and along the path, in mocking reminder, ran a border of yellow daisies.

"They ain't no trouble at all," one of the trusties was telling a companion. "Not like these nasturtiums that die out every winter. Daisies is what you call perennials, and nothin' seems to kill them. Yeah, they come up every year."

EVERY year. The phrase broke from the lips of the white-haired man as he started through the afternoon blue up the climbing road to Butternut Hill. "Yeah, they come up every year." He had watched them do it; watched them through the iron bars that shut him into his living tomb; watched them in their spring recurrence as a man might watch through each night for the promise of dawn. Routine, those little flowers were—like the work in the jute mill, the bucket-brigade, the deadly sameness of mess. Every year—like the license plates that had passed in their slow progression through his aging, prison-graying hands, 1904, 1905, 1906, 1907—

Tears of self-pity watered the old man's eyes as he hurried up the climbing road in sunlight. Thirty of those license plates—thirty years stamped out of his life—thirty years inside, looking out at nothing but a garden path of daisies that even the diluted, sooty sunlight of the prison yard couldn't kill.

They had kept him alive, those daisies. Kept him from turning into a walking corpse, hopeless, lost, moulding into a typical lifer too dead on his feet to care, too automatic to lay down and die. They had saved him from being like other cons, given him a promise of hope, assured him of a last, final vengeance at society—a fling at life—Rector's, Canfield's, Delmonico's.

Of course those places were gone now, but there were other places—Paris, maybe—racetracks—he'd take a swell bunk on a ship and swank all over the seven seas. The daisies had done that for him; kept him from forgetting the taste of life, the taste of wine and women and song. He could remember them, and he'd enjoy them again. Bottles of good whisky. The kickers on the Coast. *Daisy, Daisy*—it had been his national anthem.

"They come up every year—!" He cried it to himself as he hurried up the dusty hill. They'd be there. The bones—the diamonds would be there. Year after year his life had been there—in the bank—safe as something in a box no peterman could break. The farm the old dame had left him had remained untouched. For thirty years no man had put foot on its wide, posted fields except the tax appraisers. He'd lost it to the tax collectors at last—next week they would confiscate the property—but he'd hung on to it long enough, only selling the outlying timber land to pay off the government. What did he care if they sold it under him next week?

"They come up every year; nothin' can kill 'em—!"

As he neared the hilltop, the white-haired old man broke into a tottery, exultant run. Breath panted from his shrunken lungs and his eyes stung painfully in the afternoon brightness and the shovel in his grip weighed a ton. He wasn't as young as he'd once been—but being over sixty didn't mean anything, and all his life he'd kept in the bank, waiting for this one grand blow-off at the end. Maybe it was better this way—a fast spurt at the finish, ten years of tall living—better than a life dwindled away in little splurges that a guy wouldn't remember when he was cooked.

"It's all there waiting for me—under the daisies—!"

Freedom, money to burn, a chance to pay back society for all those unjust years. Color glowed in his wasted cheeks, his heart was pounding as if filled with new blood, he was sprinting like a man half his years when he reached the hillcrest; charged through the vine-covered Curlew gate. The weed-healed ruin of the burned mansion, the charred barn, everything had been posted against trespassers. Daisy Boy Dumont was laughing as he raced across the barnyard for a well-remembered cowpath—

"Aaaaaaaaah—!"

But only the startled crows were there to hear the scream that stopped him as he skirted the corner of the barn. Only a frightened woodchuck saw the agony that contorted his face, twisted his lips back from worn-out teeth, shrivelled his shoulders, broke him at the middle, froze him staring like a madman at the peaceful, pastured landscape below.

Next morning they found him wandering in the meadows, an unearthly, mad-eyed figure who gestured sanelessly with the shovel in his clawlike hand. They were astonished, on approaching, to hear him singing. Hoarsely voicing a ballad unheard around Four Corners for many years.

"Daisy, Daisy, give me your answer, do—!"

But the daisies wouldn't answer. Their reply was the stillness of things growing, the silence of those far-flung slopes under the morning blue. In that meadow they were countless, those hardy perennials. There were thousands of them nodding yellow heads above the richness of that earth. Acres upon acres of daisies. And if some among their myriad held a secret, they wouldn't tell.

ANY FAMILY is liable to have a skeleton in the closet—leastwise, any doctor's family. Sometimes there's more than one.

Generally the phrase implies a subject that isn't discussed beyond the Thanksgiving dinner-table; usually something scandalous, like Cousin Harry's marriage to a burlesque dancer, or something shameful, like Doc Curlew's grandson robbing the village tavern when he was sixteen and then running away to Australia after Doc had paid plenty to hush it up.

And besides that (as in the case of old Doc Curlew) there

may be the gaunt anatomical skeleton, grinny-jawed and dry-boned, such as country physicians used to keep in their office closets for study and the scaring of small boys—like the skeleton in the Curlew closet, stowed away by Gramma after the old doctor died of heart-break and she closed up his room and locked away his medical things.

ABOUT THE AUTHOR

AS A GUEST speaker at Pulpcon in Dayton, Ohio in July, 1986, I played the old Q. and A. game. I believe the opening of that game makes a good beginning for the present discussion of my fiction writing for the pulps.

Q. How and when did my fiction writing begin?

A. I have in my files the initial effort—a book entitled *The Devul and the Knight* [sic] written age five, hand-printed, hand-illustrated and hand-bound, price one cent (two copies, one remainder). The "K" circumflexed over the "night" was inserted by a brother ten years my senior. From the penny profit (from a sale within the family), I purchased a Mary Jane—taffy wrapped around a glob of peanut butter. Um.

Q. Then?

A. Shortly thereafter, I wrote, hand-printed, hand illustrated and hand-bound *Hawk Eye the Indian Boy* (two copies, price one cent, one remainder) which bought me another Mary Jane.

Q. And?

A. There followed a production entitled *The Sheriff of Red Roach Ranch*. ("Roach" was the spelling of my wicked older brother when I asked him if "Rock" was spelled with two "Ks." No matter.) I copied the spelling "Sheriff and "Ranch" from a book I was reading. Again, the one cent sale (leaving one remainder) paid for another Mary Jane.

Thus I conceived a notion.

Born was the idea that by writing I could eat.

That idea served as an apothegm for my subsequent career as a writer—a ruling not invariably a truism. As it eventuated there were times when I had Thanksgiving dinner at bottom of the totem pole at a hot dog stand.

Theodore Roscoe

However, I wrote many yarns for my high school magazine- an effort that caused an English teacher to suggest I submit a fiction effort to a magazine. Not overly optimistic, I knew I couldn't compete in a try for that day's top, the *Saturday Evening Post*. So I picked a pulp—*NorthWest Stories*. Luck! A check for $40.00! And a request for another story. This first story, "The Duel," would appear in the September 1926 issue.

That did it.

It was summertime, and I'd been a temporary P.O. employe- ee peddling mail on a route on Long Island. With a high school buddy similarly employed, who shared room and board. And I had just carried a very heavy parcel-post package addressed to a "Tillie Tisswisser," 8,001 some local avenue at the end of the line. After lugging it an extra half mile, I discovered there was no such address. Belatedly suspicious, I pried open one corner of the package and exposed a cinder block. Which my pal had wrapped and mailed with a slew of cancelled stamps.

That would have done it if my check hadn't come that day with $40.00. "I quit! I just made a fortune!" I told them at the P.O. where I dumped the cinder block. (And I got even with my buddy by ducking out of our boarding house by letting my suitcase out of our bedroom window on a clothes line and leaving him stuck with the rent.)

Anyway, the $40.00 check started me on what eventuated as a career, writing for *Action Stories, Argosy, Short Stories* and *Adventure,* for such astute editors as Jack Byrne, Don Moore and, after the war (World War II), Burroughs Mitchell and Bud Hart. Of whom I still see Bud Hart—the others no longer among those present.

World War II pretty much killed most of the now extinct pulps. From paper shortage? I can't say. But many pulp writers faded away during the war. Among them, one of the best. Frederick Faust ("Max Brand"). I'm not certain, but I believe he may have been killed at Anzio.

If one finds some astonishing names among the early pulp editors some of the writers are equally surprising. In the early *Argosy-All Story.* Mary Roberts Rinehart, Octavus Roy Cohen, Zane Gray, E. Phillips Oppenheim, John Buchan. (Buchan, who wrote "The Thirty-Nine Steps," became Governor-General of Canada.)

ONE of the questions often asked me is how did I happen to write about an old veteran yarn-spinner who spun yarns about his service in the French Foreign Legion. In North Africa back in the early '30s I encountered on a street in Casablanca this old-time Legionnaire with hashmarks up to his elbow. He agreed to talk over wine at a *brasserie.*

He didn't wear the classic old-time Legion uniform-the button-back blue overcoat, white trousers, blue cummerbund, heavy desert-boots called *brodequins.* He wore an old artillery-man's outfit. But the square-brim *kepi* with the gold torch insignia was Legion.

Questioning him in my limping French, and struggling to comprehend his metaphors, I got a *formidable* story. Aside from obvious hyperbole and manifest adjectives, some of it was perhaps true.

Here was my prototype for Thibaut Corday. Which, of course, wouldn't be his right name. You could enlist in the Legion under any name you chose, and since his right name was Hyacinth

Rastagouch, he chose Corday for what is called a *nom de guerre*. Which became your official name as a "Stepson of France." Meaning you couldn't be extradited for a crime committed elsewhere—a fact, it was said contributed to the enlistment of numerous criminals using an alias. Who knows?

Because Frenchmen can't enlist in the French Legion, I had Corday say he was a Belgian. Or was it a Swiss? Anyway, the teller of my story attributed to Corday good English, partly translated.

Since his yarns were obviously mixtures of fact and fiction, I never presumed they would be taken seriously by the reader. And was surprised when several critics wrote to tell me the military tactics in this or that Corday tale were hokum. They were so intended to sound.

Incidentally, some Legion veterans in New York voted me an honorary member of the Veterans of the French Foreign Legion.

Actually, I never saw the Legion in combat. At a Legion H.Q. back in Sidi Bel Abbes, I was querying one of the officers. Apparently he thought I was planning to enlist. He shook his head at me with the comment: *"Discipline terrible!"* They followed the old rule, *"March qu creve."* "March or die." If a Legionnaire fell out, exhausted, in a Sahara march, they sent a sharpshooter back to kill him, and spare him from torture by desert tribesmen. But the Legionnaires I saw in action weren't risking their lives.

In Europe back then there was a saying. When the English conquer a country they build a custom house. The Germans build a fort. The French build a road. Back then (the '30s) the Legionnaires I saw in action were covered with not-very-glamorous dust, wielding picks and shovels building a road. Some of them in barracks slept in cots with the cot-legs in cans filled with water, to defeat scorpions. Their pay, if I recall correctly, afforded them a daily bottle of *pinard* (cheap red wine).

Nothing so intriguing, colorful and lively as in such novels as *Beau Geste.*

So don't join the French Foreign Legion today. You'd get a plain khaki uniform, and risk only being bored to death.

Still, you'd learn one thing. Watch them, if chance occurs, on parade in France or on TV. There's no military outfit anywhere that can out-march their particular step.

ASIDE from the Foreign Legion, I most enjoyed writing for *Action Stories* a series about an adventurer named Peter Scarlet. There were at least 14 Peter Scarlet stories, beginning with "Jungle Joker" in the May 1927 issue of *Action Stories*. Other favorites were a tale entitled "On Account of a Woman" (*Adventure*, January 1936) and a tale for *Argosy*, "The Voodoo Express" (October 10,1931).

On another tack, I enjoyed writing a series for *Argosy* titled "Four Corners," which began with "He Took Richmond" in the June 5, 1937 issue of *Argosy*. These were adventures experienced by a youngster whose uncle was Sheriff in a small town about 100 miles from New York. One of the early Four Corners stories was "I Was the Kid With the Drum" (October 30, 1937)—a murder mystery. They used to have a kid aid the drummer by carrying in a parade the front end of a big base drum (guess where the body was concealed in a hurry by the murderer in this case). Of course, the drum seemed heavier than usual. And the drum-beat seemed more of a thump than the usual vibratory boom. The kid in the story didn't get it. But anyway the murderous drummer discovered he'd killed the wrong person.

In another "Four Corners" tale, I had a thief change his money into coins—loot he could bury in a well. Okay? But when he went back to safely get and spend this big bag of coins, he was trapped by the fact the silver dollars all bore the same date-the date of the robbery.

In one of my favorite Four Corners stories, "Frivolous Sal" (*Argosy,* July 17, 1937), the small town gentry were worried because it was rumored the young woman, so named (after a popular song), kept a diary. Fruitless efforts were made to get hold of it. In the end? Try to guess it.

I had a lot of fun writing "The Head," which appeared in *Short Stories,* December 10, 1932. As a stringer reporter, I had gone to Panama to investigate rumors of "White Indians" in the remote interior near the Colombian border. At a bar in Cristobal I asked the bar-keep if he'd heard of these Indians. Overhearing my query, a bar-fly character asked if I was interred in Jiboro Indians—the tribe that, through a mysterious process, boned, cured and somehow shrank human heads to the size of a baseball. (Origin of the term "head-shrinker" for a psychologist.) The bar-fly said he had one to sell, and produced what appeared to be a much-shrunken human head. As the Jiboro Indians actually beheaded their enemies and with incredible artsy-crafty skill created such curiosities, I was interested in the specimen handed me by the bar-fly. Ah! Only $300.00.

But the bartender, behind his hand, winked at me a negative signal. I didn't buy the head.

When the bar-fly indignantly took off with his allegedly shrunken head, the bartender advised me it was a fake, a monkey head fixed up to look human.

Later I saw an authentic shrunken head on display in another bar.

When World War II put an end to my pulp efforts, by good luck I sold *Only in New England*—a novel I'd intended for *Argosy*—to Scribner's. Surprisingly, it made the Literary Guild Book of the Month.

Thereafter, I wrote two Navy histories—*U.S. Submarine Operations, World War II* (1949) and *U.S. Destroyer Operations, World War II* (1953) which were published by the Naval Institute at Annapolis (and are still on the market). I also wrote *This is Your Navy* (1950) for service reading. This was followed by *The Web of Conspiracy* (1959), about the Lincoln assassination, which became a *DuPont Show of the Month* on TV in 1961. Of which, with a great deal of help from my devoted wife, Rosa-mond, got me going again in fiction.

Today I can't recall what some of these tall tales written 50 years ago were about. Maybe I should have written some of them under an assumed name. But when I wrote them I felt I should take my lumps if, compared to many of early *Argosy's* great writers, my efforts proved mediocre. And on the other hand, if some drew plaudits, I'd like to take a bow in person.

Brave, no?

THE ARGOSY LIBRARY ™

SERIES 1 INCLUDES:

* DENT * KETCHUM * KLINE *
* MacISAAC * ROSCOE *
* ROUSSEAU *
* SELTZER *
* TUTTLE *
* WIRT *
WORTS

THE BEST FICTION
FROM THE FRANK
A. MUNSEY LINE

THE ARGOSY LIBRARY

GENIUS JONES
BY THE CO-CREATOR OF DOC SAVAGE
LESTER DENT

THE ARGOSY LIBRARY

WHEN TIGERS ARE HUNTING
THE COMPLETE ADVENTURES OF GORDIE, SOLDIER OF FORTUNE: VOLUME 1
W. WIRT

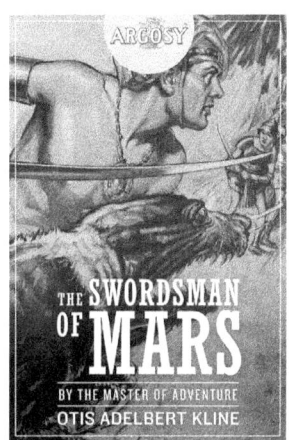

ARGOSY

THE SWORDSMAN OF MARS
BY THE MASTER OF ADVENTURE
OTIS ADELBERT KLINE

THE ARGOSY LIBRARY

THE SHERLOCK OF SAGELAND
THE COMPLETE TALES OF SHERIFF HENRY: VOLUME 1
W.C. TUTTLE

THE ARGOSY LIBRARY

GONE NORTH
BY ARGOSY READERS' FAVORITE
CHARLES ALDEN SELTZER

THE ARGOSY LIBRARY

THE MASKED MASTER MIND
BY THE AUTHOR OF PETER THE BRAZEN
GEORGE F. WORTS

ARGOSY

BALATA
BY THE AUTHOR OF THE RAMBLER
FRED MacISAAC

ARGOSY

BRET-WALDA
BY ARGOSY READERS' FAVORITE
PHILIP KETCHUM

ARGOSY

DRAFT OF ETERNITY
BY THE CREATOR OF JIM ANTHONY
VICTOR ROUSSEAU

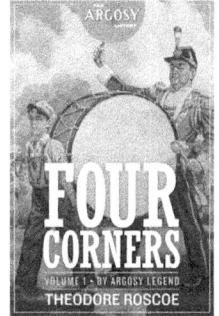

ARGOSY

FOUR CORNERS
VOLUME 1 • BY ARGOSY LEGEND
THEODORE ROSCOE

SERIES 1 • AVAILABLE SPRING 2015

www.ingramcontent.com/pod-product-compliance
Lightning Source LLC
Chambersburg PA
CBHW051831020726
47502CB00005B/1736